Finding the Captain

by
James Hume

Finding the Captain

Copyright © 2022, Jim McCallum Publishing Ltd. (JMPL)

Editing by JMPL

Cover Design by Victoria Bushby

Book Design by JMPL

Thanks to John Pilkington for historic police procedures and Scots law

First JMPL electronic publication: 25 February, 2023

English Edition
ISBN No: 9798378916016
Published in the UK by Jim McCallum Publishing Ltd, 2023.

.

.

For

DOUGLAS and LINDA

My fine brother and

Sister-in-law!

Part 1
1946

Chapter 1. Oleg Petrov

Oleg Petrov always won. His father demanded it. And he delivered. Even if it was unfair on the other party. Tough. But that's what life was all about. Be nice on the surface, but win.

His turning point had come in 1912. He'd just joined the board of his father's small bank in Saint Petersburg, Russia, and wanted to expand the business faster. He searched for great people to invest in. Those with big ideas and a passion to succeed.

Iosef Jugashvili was just such a man. Mid-thirties. Stocky, with a moustache. Smart, with a passion for the rights of working people. Wanted help to upgrade his weekly Zvezta into a daily called Pravda. To spread his message more widely.

Oleg's father had warned him off politics. Too much dirt. Too much rage. Never a good deal. But this man seemed unique. So Oleg backed him.

Iosef edited the new paper, and used the pen name, Stalin, meaning steel man. Then took it as his surname for the rest of his life. Years later, he became Leader of the Soviet Union, ever grateful to Oleg, who became part of his inner circle.

In Stalin's wake, the small bank grew to have an HQ in Moscow near Red Square. Oleg became very wealthy and influential. This shielded his family from daily Russian life. But now, in 1946, his sister's boy, Sergei, working in Warsaw, Poland, had gone missing in the UK, and no one seemed to be doing anything.

So Oleg shouted loudly. To the Soviet Ambassador in London, and his key man, Vadim Lenkov. 'What the hell's going on over there? What are you doing about finding our Sergei?'

'I'm sorry, sir. It's the weekend, but we have no record of Sergei in London. If he was here on official business, we would know about it. He must have come on a personal visit.'

'Well, bloody well find out.'

'I will, sir. I'll call Warsaw on Monday and get details of his visit. We'll take it from there.'

On Wednesday, Oleg received a copy of a report on Sergei by a senior police officer in Glasgow. A note from Lenkov asked him to call once he'd read it. His daughter Nadya, who acted as his PA, brought it into him. He read it through.

'Report by Special Branch, Glasgow, in response to requests from Soviet Embassies to the Foreign Office.

Background (from FO notes)

On Monday, 15 July, 1946, SB London asked us to investigate the disappearance of an employee at the Soviet Embassy, London. He had not returned as planned from a business trip to Glasgow. The man, Anatoly Golovkin, works in internal security. He also has diplomatic immunity.

They thought he flew to Glasgow on Wednesday, 10 July, on the evening BEA flight. But no one of that name flew on that flight. So he may have travelled by train. He called the Embassy on Thursday to check messages, and confirmed he would return next day. Concern grew when he had not returned by Friday evening.

He had left a contact number in Glasgow, South 3819. Over the weekend, Embassy staff called it. They found it was a rented villa occupied by a family from London from Friday. They gave the Embassy the contact number for the lawyers that handled the rental. Western 6136, another Glasgow number.

The lawyers said they had rented the villa for two nights from Wednesday to a Mr John Clark, and gave his contact number, Kelvin 4395. They tried to call this number, but found it inactive.

The Embassy then asked the FO for help. They passed the request to SB London, and it then came to us.

The same morning, the FO also received a request from the British Embassy in Warsaw, to check on an employee of the Soviet Embassy there also missing last week. This man, Sergei Yushkov, worked in internal security, and might have flown to London. Since the two cases were similar, the FO also sent us that info.

Findings

Our team contacted the lawyers, who said, other than John Clark, they did not know of anyone else staying over that rental period. However, they gave us details for the ladies that ran a villa cleaning and breakfast service.

We interviewed the ladies. They told us that Mr Clark and two other men had stayed in the villa last week from Wednesday. The men had left the villa on Friday morning as agreed.

They confirmed the photos we had from the Soviet Embassies in London and Warsaw, were indeed the two men. On Friday, they deep cleaned the villa, to prepare it for a new party arriving that evening.

They said Mr Clark called the men Peter and Marius. Like Marius Goring the film actor.

We then checked with BEA at Renfrew Airport to see if two men called Peter and Marius were booked on the Friday morning flight to London.

They confirmed there was a Mariusz Kujawska, a Polish national, and a Peter Smith, a UK national, both listed as 'No Show'. Both had arrived in Glasgow on the Wednesday evening flight from London.

BEA then checked their booking records. Star Travel of Kensington had booked flights Warsaw to London to Glasgow return for Mariusz, and flights London to Glasgow return for Peter. All paid for in cash.

We concluded that Mr Golovkin had travelled from London using the Peter Smith ID, and Mr Yushkov had used the Mariusz Kujawska ID. We assume the Embassy staff did not know they travelled on false IDs.

The ladies at the house had said the men's car had a 'Central Car Rental' sticker on the rear window. This company confirmed John Clark had rented a car from Wednesday to Friday morning. He had shown passport and driving licence IDs. We found these IDs, and his contact details, were false.

During the rental, the car logged 124 miles, and returned early on Friday morning before the office opened, with the keys dropped through the letter box.

We therefore conclude, on this evidence, that the two Russian men visited Glasgow last week from Wednesday evening to Friday morning to meet an unknown local man. The use of false IDs suggests they met to plan or commit a crime. But checks so far have found no such men charged with any crime.

Clearly, the Russians' return plans changed. They did not travel on any other flight from Glasgow, though they could have travelled by train.

We will continue our checks, but feel this trail has now gone cold. If the Embassies can provide more data on the men's plans and activities in the Glasgow area, we will follow up and report back.

Regarding diplomatic immunity. Under the Congress of Vienna, this is only valid for registered people on official duties using their real names.

Signed: Alexandra Maxwell, CS, SB Glasgow
Date: 15 July, 1946'

'Have you read this, Nadya? Do you believe it?'

'Not sure, dad. I talked to Lenkov on Monday. He still didn't know about Sergei. Said his man Golovkin was also missing. And even though this man handled internal security for the Embassy, they now realise they knew nothing about him. Strange.'

'Shit. Get me Lenkov on the phone.'

He came on the line. 'You've got the report, sir?'

'I have, and it's not a pleasant read. This Glasgow man, John Clark, must have set it up to meet Golovkin. And that wouldn't just be one way.

'So, Golovkin must have Clark's phone number. Dig deep to find it. Bring in a team of top private detectives to find his real name. I'll pay for it. It's the only way we'll break this.

'And what's this comment at the end about diplomatic immunity? What does that mean?'

'Well, we're saying that Sergei and Golovkin were covered by DI, sir, but she's saying they're not. Because they used false names.'

'And what does the Congress of Vienna say?'

'We think it applies. But it's a grey area, sir.'

'Remember, we're the Soviet Union. The most powerful country in the world. If we say it applies, then that's it. No arguments. Keep in touch. Goodbye.'

He hung up and grimaced. 'Lenkov sounds soft, Nadya. Keep the pressure on him.'

'Will do, dad.'

'Tell me more about Sergei. I don't really know the lad very well. But you and Dmitri played with him out at the dacha when you were young.'

'Yeah. I always thought he was a bit sinister. He'd lost the tip of his fourth finger in a bicycle accident. Then fell out of a tree that left a scar on his right temple. So he thought he was ugly, and reacted against beauty.'

'In what way?'

'One day a butterfly landed on the table in the garden. I said it was so beautiful. He just scooped it up, tore its wings off, and squashed it. Then laughed at me. Nasty. I didn't really like him.'

'Well, like him or not, he's part of our family. We need to help him. Though with his NKGB training, I suppose he could well do something criminal. But why would he vanish and not travel back?'

'People like him don't vanish, dad. Somebody took him or killed him. And I doubt someone killed him. Sergei was trained to kill with the NKGB. Killing him would leave a trace the police couldn't ignore.

'So, dad, why would two tough men fly to Glasgow and meet with a local man? All using false names? The report suggests they planned or committed a crime. And that's probably right.

'Now we know Sergei does not speak good English. Whatever they did must take two of them to complete. Otherwise Golovkin could do it on his own.

'Why does he need Sergei? I know he's my cousin, but he doesn't have too many talents. In fact, his only talent is killing.

'I think Golovkin brought Sergei over to kill someone. For big money. And the local man organised it. It's the only thing that makes sense.

'And remember, dad? When we were over in the UK in the thirties buying property? The one thing we learned was that the Brits were very clever at using the English language to disguise what they were saying.

'Look at some of the problems we had with the properties after we bought them. And when we queried them, they pointed out they'd explained everything we asked about. And we had to cover these extra costs.

'I think this police report might be the same. What they say in the report is true. But it responds only to the

10

question Lenkov asked. We have two people missing. Can you investigate? And that's what they've done. But maybe we didn't ask the right question?

'We should also have asked if they knew *why* they went missing. For example, she says no such men were charged. But the police arrest someone and then charge him. Why didn't she say no such men were arrested? So no, I don't trust that report, dad.

'Sergei and Golovkin could have been arrested but not yet charged for some reason. So her report is true. But they're still holding our guys somewhere. And the only way to free them is to hold two of theirs and swap.'

'Good thinking, Nadya. So, how do we do that?'

'We use my brother, Dmitri. He's also ex-NKGB but on the strategic side. He could lift two Brits and hold them in one of our properties. Then fix the swap.'

'What if it's not Brits? What if it's Americans?'

'Americans? Why would they get involved in something like this in the UK?'

He shrugged. 'It's the sort of thing they might do.'

'Well, okay. Let's line up two Americans and two Brits. Once the detectives tell us which it is, we go into action. Could they trace us via the properties?'

'No. We bought them through the British Virgin Islands company. So there's no trace.'

'Let me just check them, dad. I'll get the plans.' She left the room and was back in a few minutes. 'We have the apartment block near Hyde Park. Two apartments are vacant, awaiting new rentals. But I think it's too difficult to hold two prisoners there. Too much movement.

'Then we have the two Nash Terrace houses at Regent's Park. One of them is awaiting a new rental, so we could use that. It also has two bedrooms on the lower ground floor we could use for the prisoners.

'And we have our staff available to service it. Also, we can access it via the mews at the back. I think that would work, dad.'

'Okay, get hold of Dmitri, and brief him on what we want. And call Lenkov and tell him we want Dmitri in on all his meetings. Let's do it. Let's get Sergei back.'

***

Dmitri Petrov got things done. He modelled himself on his father, who used him as a trouble-shooter within the bank. To fix wayward customers one way or the other.

They mostly found the money owed. But where they didn't, Dmitri closed them, took over their assets, then sold or restructured the business within an offshoot of the bank. Tough on the owners, but good for the bank.

Nadya knocked on his open door. 'Got a minute?'

'Sure.' He rose from his desk and waved her to an easy chair on the other side of his office.

She closed the door and sat. 'Do you know Sergei's gone missing in the UK?'

'Yeah. Dad mentioned it last night.'

'Well, we've just got a copy of a police report on the disappearance of Sergei and a man called Golovkin from the London Embassy. Here, have a read at it.'

He took the document and read it through. Then looked over at Nadya. 'Do we have any idea what Sergei was doing over there?'

'No. But you know Sergei. Probably something criminal, like she says. But he's family, and dad wants him back.' She went through her analysis of the report. 'Dad's told Lenkov, the Chief at our London Embassy, to find out what he can about the local man, John Clark. To bring in private detectives. We'll pay for it.

'But he wants you across there to run this. Lenkov is a career diplomat, and dad thinks he's too soft. We'll tell him you have to be at any meetings on the case.

'It's possible the police might be holding our two for some reason. And the only way we'll get them back is to barter them for two of theirs. So dad wants you to identify two Brits and two Americans that you can lift once we know who's got our men. The woman who wrote the report would be a good start point.

'The Nash Terrace house B is free, and you can stay there and hold the prisoners in the basement. But don't tell Lenkov what you're doing.'

'Okay, but what about our secret stuff? We avoid going to the Embassy because if it.'

'This is family business, Dmitri. Takes priority.'

Right. Leave it with me.'

'*Udachi*. Best of luck.'

***

On Friday morning, Dmitri met Vadim Lenkov in his office at the Soviet Embassy in London. They sat together at the conference table. 'Welcome to London, Mister Petrov. Hope your visit is successful.'

Lenkov looked nervous. He clearly knew who was now in charge of this case. 'I do too. Call me Dmitri.'

'Thank you. As Nadya suggested, we have arranged a cover story for your visit. You're a colleague from our Embassy in Warsaw. Name of Dmitri Bardin, who is a real under-secretary there if anyone should check. Here to look after their interests in the matter. Which is in fact true. I hope that's okay.'

'Yes, it's fine. Where are we with finding a phone number for this John Clark person in Glasgow?'

'After two days searching every note in Golovkin's office and room, we found an entry in an old desk diary,

"JC K 374". We think this might be Clark's number. So, as your father suggested, we called in a firm of private detectives to follow up on it.

'It's a company called PL Investigations, who do a lot of work for our legal advisors here. The head of the company, Paul Lynch, will be here shortly. So, your visit is very timely.'

'Good. So, tell me about your man, Golovkin.'

'Anatoly joined us here about a year ago as Head of Internal Security. But we now realise we know very little about him.

'I believe he's ex-NKGB, and may have a senior role over such staff in our Western Europe Embassies.'

'According to the police report, he went to Glasgow using a false name. Do you know why?'

'We don't, Dmitri. I assume it was to keep his off-site activities secret.'

'Criminal activities? Is that likely?'

Lenkov spread his hands. 'We just don't know.'

'And what about Sergei Yushkov?'

'We did not know he was here. And he also travelled under a false name. Nadya said he's your cousin.'

'That's correct. Hence our active interest.'

'Yes, I understand.' His phone rang and he picked up. 'Good. Please show him in.' He hung up. 'That's Paul Lynch here.'

Dmitri sat back.

Lenkov's secretary showed in a medium-sized man. He looked fit, with greying hair, and a large warm smile. 'Morning, gentlemen. I'm Paul Lynch. Good to meet you. Looking forward to working with you.'

Lenkov went across and shook hands. 'Morning, Mr Lynch. I'm Vadim Lenkov, Chief of the Embassy. And this is Mr Dmitri Bardin, who represents the interests of our Embassy in Warsaw, Poland, in the matter.'

Dmitri rose and shook hands. 'Morning, Mr Lynch.'

'Ach, just call me Paul. It's a lot easier.'

'Okay, Paul. Please, sit here, and tell us about your background and how you might help us.'

'I will indeed. Here's my card. I started my career as a Garda officer in Dublin. That's the Irish Police and Security Service. I'd always wanted to be a cop, and I was good at it. In fact, at one stage, I was the youngest Inspector in the Dublin force.

'But, you know, Dublin's a small city, and Ireland's a small country, and it all just became too routine. Lost the spark. Career prospects limited. Then one day, I met a mate, an ex-cop, and he changed my life.

'He'd left the Garda, and started up on his own as a private detective. Had good contacts among lawyers and did pretty well. He'd just done a successful job for the lawyers of a foreign embassy in Dublin, and they wanted him to do the same job for the London embassy.

'But he didn't want to go for family reasons, and suggested that I would be ideal if I moved to London.

'I talked to the wife, the lawyers, the embassy, and decided to go for it. We moved to London just over ten years ago now.

'The lawyers helped me get a licence and set up the business, and we've done really well since. We focus on working with foreign embassies.

'We have a small team in London, and alliances with high quality PDs around the country. I believe your lawyers put in a good word for me, and I'm happy to help. Whatever the job. And keep it secret.'

Lenkov cut in. 'On that point, Paul, could I ask you to sign this Confidential Agreement, please?'

Lynch read it through and signed it. 'No problem. And I have one for you too.'

Lenkov read it and signed. 'Thank you, Paul. Our case starts with this report from the UK police. Perhaps you'd read it and then we can discuss it.'

15

Lynch took the document and read it. 'I take it you'd like me to find out what happened to your men?'

'That's correct. And here are their photos. We think the key is to identify the local man. He must have set up this meeting with Golovkin. We've carried out a deep search of Golovkin's papers and found what might be the man's phone number. Here it is.'

Lynch studied the paper. 'Is this all you've got?'

'That's all we can find, so far.'

'Okay. We'll start with that. But it may take a bit of digging. Could take a few weeks.'

'Well, as soon as you can, please. How do you charge your time?'

'By the hour. The rate depends on the seniority of the investigator.' He went into his briefcase. 'This gives you the rates. Our people have to justify every minute of their time. Any expenses are charged at cost.'

Lenkov passed the sheet to Dmitri. 'Mr Bardin will pay for your time. So, you'll need to satisfy him.'

Dmitri took the document. A one-page flyer, with a picture of a deerstalker hat at the top, and giving his company's information.

'PL INVESTIGATIONS – OUR ABC

Analytical – the right conclusions from the evidence
B
Confident – we'll find it if it exists
Diligent – we dig deeper
Efficient – every hour a good hour

Rates – Investigator – 2/6 per hour
      Senior Investigator – 5/- per hour
      Director – 7/6 per hour
      Plus Expenses (travel, meals, hotels, etc.)
      Plus Witness Expenses (if any)

Invoiced weekly against timesheets – Pay weekly
Payments in Advance get 20% more hours

B? – The Best in the Business'

Dmitri smiled. Good summary. He liked this man.
Could do business with him. 'Fine. I'm happy with that.'

'Good. I'll get started right away. Do you want to
pay in advance?'

'Yeah. Sounds better value. How much?'

He thought for a moment. 'Maybe three weeks? Say
thirty pounds? We'll repay any excess, of course.'

'Okay.' Dmitri counted out the cash from his wallet,
and Paul gave him a receipt.

'Thank you very much, gentlemen. Good doing
business with you. Contact me any time on that number
on the flyer. May I have your contact numbers, please?'

Lenkov gave him a card. 'Get me any time.'

Dmitri smiled. 'When I'm over here, I travel a lot.
So leave any messages with Jill Graham, my assistant at
Barclays. Here's her number.'

'I'll do that.'

They all stood and shook hands. Dmitri said, 'I'll
walk out with you, Paul. I've got to get over to the City.'

Lenkov showed them out, and they walked together
into Bayswater Road.

Dmitri stopped. 'Got a minute, Paul? I'd like you to
do another job for me. Secret. In parallel to this one.'

'Okay. How can I help?'

'The woman who wrote that police report, CS
Alexandra Maxwell. Could you find out all about her?
Where she lives? Where she goes? What she does? Is
she married? Friends? Social life?'

'Yeah, I can. Based in Glasgow, though. But I've
got a very good man there. Do you want photos?'

'Yes, please. You okay checking a police officer?'

Paul scoffed. 'Dmitri, I'm Irish. I have no loyalty to the Brits. Or to the Americans. Or any of them. I do a private job. Get paid. That's it. That's me.'

'Good. So how much are we talking about?'

'Mmm. Maybe another thirty?'

'Okay.' He counted out the money, and Paul gave him another receipt. 'Don't mention this to Lenkov.'

'Understood. Lips sealed.'

He patted Paul's shoulder. 'Good man. *Udachi.*'

'What's that?'

'Oh, it's a family word. Means best of luck. By the way, my name isn't Bardin. That's just a cover for this job. If you want me via Jill, ask for Dmitri Petrov. She'll get a message to me.'

'Fine. No problem.'

Paul went off towards his office, and Dmitri headed for the City. Then he'd spend much of the weekend with Jill. Divorced and lonely. In her thirties and pleasant. He'd had an affair with her on previous visits, and she loved his attentions. Then, back to Moscow on Monday. Job done. Or at least, started.

***

Dmitri drove his taxi along Birdcage Walk, and pulled up behind another taxi parked under the tress in the dark. Outside a large office block. Meeting place for Mikhail, the Military Attaché at the Embassy.

He joined him leaning against his taxi, both dressed in gabardine coats and caps, for all the world just two cab drivers waiting for their fares from the office.

'Hi Mikhail. Got your message.' They shook hands.

'Thanks for coming, Dmitri. I almost shit myself when I saw you with Lenkov this morning. We agreed you wouldn't come into the Embassy.'

'Well, it wasn't to discuss our business, Mikhail. It was family business.'

'What family business?'

'Two of our men went missing in Glasgow last week. I'm sure you've heard about it.'

Oh, yeah. You mean Golovkin and someone from Warsaw Embassy?'

'That's right. The man from Warsaw is my cousin. And dad's going nuts because no one in London seems to do anything about it. I'm over to fix that.'

'I see. That makes sense now.'

'It won't compromise our arrangements, Mikhail.'

'I know. It was just such a surprise.'

'Anyway, how are our cash streams going?'

'Doing well. We now have three spy groups running, and getting some great info on the Brits' secret work. Some of it from the US.

'Do you know Deputy PM Beria took over our atomic bomb project after we got blindsided by the Americans in Japan last year?'

'Yeah, I heard that.'

'He's hacked out a lot of our dead wood and got spies into the centre of the US nuclear programme.

'We might get one of these top spies over here, so we'll need to set up another stream for that.'

'No problem. Just let me know when.'

'Well, I assume it'll come from the top. Beria will contact your father.'

'Okay. That's fine. Good seeing you again.'

'Yeah, good to see you, Dmitri. Take care.'

'Will do. *Udachi*.'

***

Three weeks later, Dmitri met Lenkov again in his office. Lenkov looked even more nervous than before. 'What do you think of Lynch, Vadim?'

'I think he's found it quite difficult, Dmitri. He's given me weekly updates, which I've passed on to you. Seems to me slow progress, though. But they may not be on it full time if it has to fit in with other work.'

'That's true. We'll soon find out.'

A few minutes later, the secretary showed Paul Lynch into the room. 'Morning, gentlemen. Good to see you again.' They all stood and shook hands. 'A tricky wee job you gave me, for sure.'

Lenkov raised his eyebrows. 'Why's that?'

'First, the possible phone number, K374. Thought it would be in Scotland. But then discovered 382 towns or villages listed there with an initial K.

'We then asked the operator for each in turn with the number 374. Of these, 227 had an exchange, 73 used a three-digit number, and four had an active 374. Only one was near Glasgow, Kilmaurs, so we started there.

'We called the number twenty times over the next two days, at all times of the day and night, and never got a reply. So, our man in Glasgow went to Kilmaurs, got a copy of the local phone directory, and scanned it line by line to find the address of that number.

'And he didn't find it. Must be ex-directory. So he bought a detailed map of the village that showed each house as a block, some of them with a house number.

'He then went through the local directory again, and marked each listed number on the map with a red dot. There were 103 of these. He then looked for large houses that didn't have a red dot. These would be people who could afford a phone, but wanted to remain ex-directory. And there were three.

'He got the precise address of these three properties. Then looked up the electoral roll in the library to get the names of the occupants. McKenzie, Houston and Muir. If he was right, then one of them would be the false John Clark. And the house must be empty because the number kept ringing out.

'From neighbours he found the only house that fitted was Muir's. The neighbour there told him that on a Thursday night a month ago, July 11, the police had come to Muir's house, moved the family out to the wife's mother's house, and spent a couple of days searching the house. No one knew why. Then Mr Muir died on the Monday in a Glasgow hospital. She showed him the local paper that carried a photo of Mr Muir with the death notice. The wife has still not returned, though she turns up for work each day at the school next door.

'Our man got a copy of the local paper for that week. And this morning, went to see the two ladies who had provided breakfast service at the villa in Glasgow. They confirmed the photo of Muir was John Clark.

'So, as of this minute, we have at last matched the false John Clark to the real Norman Muir. A lawyer who ran a legal business from his home in Kilmaurs, and whom your men met in Glasgow. I assume you want us to find out what happened next?'

Dmitri nodded. 'Good piece of work, Paul.'

'Yeah, it is. Our man in Glasgow is very sound.'

'Okay, Paul. We'd like you to keep going. How long do you think it will take?'

Paul shrugged. 'Don't know. How long is a piece of string? The only thing we know at this point from the police report is that the men's rental car travelled 124 miles. So, I'd say, maybe three more weeks?'

'Right. Is that another thirty pounds?'

'Yeah. We'll return any excess, of course'

'Fine.' Dmitri counted out the notes, and Paul gave him a receipt. 'Let's meet again here three weeks today.' He turned to Lenkov. 'Is that okay with you, Vadim?'

21

'Of course.'

'Let's make sure we keep this secret. Thank you.' He stood and shook hands. 'I've got another meeting at Barclays, so I'll walk you out, Paul.'

Dmitri and Paul left and walked up the Bayswater Road towards the tube station. 'How did you get on with the other job, Paul? Tracking the Maxwell woman?'

'So far, so good. Our man up there has a contact in Glasgow Police, who'd heard she lived in a big house in the West End.

He checked the phone directory and found her home listed under her father's name. Here's a photo of her leaving home one morning.'

Dmitri studied the photo. Tall, quite attractive, and determined looking.

'I'm told she's a tough lady who runs a tight ship. But now promoted to Scotland Yard, here in London. We checked local hotels, and here are photos of her leaving the Charing Cross Hotel and in Trafalgar Square the other morning.

'She dines each evening with a different man. I think maybe to better know her new senior staff? But I expect her hotel stay is short-term. Do you want me to keep going with this?'

'Yes, please. I'd like to build a picture of where she stays, where she goes, and with whom. So keep it going for at least another three weeks. Another thirty pounds?'

Paul smiled and nodded. Dmitri counted out the notes, and Paul gave him another receipt.

'Thanks very much, Paul. Look forward to seeing you again in three weeks. *Udachi*.''

'Yeah, udachi. Thanks.' They shook hands.

***

Again, three weeks later, the three of them met in Lenkov's office.

Paul Lynch launched into his feedback. 'I can now tell you what happened to your two men on July 11. And I'll explain it in three sections.

'First, my official report. Which is what we know, backed up by witness statements. I've given you all the details in this anonymous report, which you can pass on to other parties.

'Second, what we don't know, and probably never find out. You'd need to get that info from elsewhere.

'Third, what we think might have happened, but can't prove it. Is that okay?'

Dmitri and Lenkov nodded. 'That's fine.'

'The last time we met, our man in Glasgow had just confirmed that the photo of a local man, Norman Muir, who died in a Glasgow hospital on Monday, July 15, was indeed the false John Clark. A real breakthrough.

'We then checked the Glasgow papers around the same period. The *Daily Record* carried a brief article in the previous Saturday paper. This is it.'

Dmitri read it. "Wealthy legal eagle Norman Muir, 42, subject of an attack in Gallowgate last Monday, is fighting for his life in the Western Infirmary after another attack at a house in Rhu on Thursday.

A USAAF helicopter in the area airlifted him to the hospital. Police enquiries are ongoing."

Dmitri passed it to Lenkov. 'Tough life, huh?'

'Yeah. The Monday incident happened before your men got to Glasgow on the Wednesday. It seemed an argument over football teams turned violent. So, it's not relevant to our report.

'However, the fact that Muir was brought to hospital in a USAAF helicopter is very relevant. We've never heard of that happening before.

'We went to the hospital, and found a nurse who had treated Muir. He had two cracked ribs and a severe head injury. She said he had a round-the-clock police guard, because they didn't know why he had been attacked, and might still be in danger.

'She'd also asked the police about the helicopter, and was told that it was in the area testing equipment for tracking submarines, and agreed to an urgent request from the police to airlift Muir.'

'That was handy, huh?'

'Sure was, Dmitri. So we went to Rhu to find out what happened there. It's a small village on Gare Loch, about twenty-five miles west of Glasgow.

'We found that on Thursday, July 11, there had been some sort of fight at a cottage next to a hotel, and police and an ambulance were called. A helicopter then airlifted a seriously injured man from the front lawn of the hotel, which ties in with what the nurse said.

'By asking around, we met a waiter at the hotel who saw it all happen. A brilliant witness. He's a lad from London, going to Cambridge this year, and he and his girlfriend took a working holiday at the hotel.

'He says that when the helicopter arrived at their front lawn, everybody ran out to see it. No one had ever seen one before. A tall man in a flying suit got out and walked down towards a cottage on the loch side.

'About twenty minutes later, an ambulance brought an injured man on a stretcher to the aircraft, and the man in the flying suit helped load him into it. He assumed they took the injured man to a local hospital. He thought it was just after half-past two.

'The helicopter came back and took off three more times at roughly half-hour intervals. The next two times, it also loaded an injured man on a stretcher. He assumed it also took these two men to hospital.

'The last flight by the helicopter picked up the tall man in the flying suit.

'Our detective checked back with the Glasgow hospital, but they received only one man by helicopter. He checked all the other hospitals nearby, but none had dealt with anyone in a helicopter.

'Our man also checked with the woman who handles the cottage rentals, and she confirmed the newspaper pic as John Clark, who had rented the cottage for two nights.

'So, from this evidence, we're sure that Norman Muir, aka John Clark, and your two Russians were at that cottage on Thursday, July 11. And all three were airlifted out by USAAF helicopter. Muir went to hospital in Glasgow, but we don't know where they took your men. The nearest USAAF airbase at the time was at Prestwick, about thirty miles away across the Clyde estuary. But it closed at the end of July.

'We think you should go back to CS Maxwell with this info and ask her to recheck the case, and see what she and her team come back with.'

Dmitri glanced over at Lenkov. 'What do you think, Vadim? Happy with that?'

'Well, I'm happy we now know a lot more. It's a good piece of work, Paul, and we appreciate it. But I'm not happy if the Americans have grabbed our men, and haven't told us yet after seven weeks. That's bad news.'

Dmitri nodded. 'You're right. But I suggest you call her today with the main points, and demand a meeting with her first thing Monday. I'll come with you.'

'Okay, I'll do that.'

'Good. Now, Paul. You've told us what you know, and what you don't know. What else do you have?'

'Right. First things first. Our waiter witness says the helicopter made four lifts from the hotel lawn at roughly thirty-minute intervals. That's why he assumed it took the injured men to a local hospital.

'But we know that's not true. The first flight took the injured man, Muir, to the Western Infirmary in Glasgow, twenty-five miles away.

'Now, these helicopters fly at about sixty miles per hour. A mile a minute. So that first flight to the hospital in Glasgow could not possibly return in thirty minutes. It would take the thick end of an hour for that round trip.

'So, our witness assumed one helicopter. But we think there were actually two. It's the only way they could have done the lifts half-an-hour apart. And that changes the whole picture.

'The police told the nurse the helicopter was in the area and had agreed to fly the man to hospital at their request. But if there were two helicopters, it would take a whole different level of resource and management. They would need to plan for it well in advance. And we think that's what happened.

'The first lift was the injured man to hospital in the first helicopter. The second was one of your men sedated on a stretcher taken to the USAAF base at Prestwick in the second helicopter. The third was your other man to the same airbase in the first helicopter, now back from hospital. And the fourth was the second helicopter back to take the tall man in the flying suit to his airbase.

'The question then, is why? What were the men doing at that cottage? And we think we know the answer. But you won't like it.'

Dmitri raised his eyebrows. 'Tell us anyway.'

'Okay. The rentals woman told us John Clark had rented the cottage for two nights for his cousin.

'She met the cousin when she gave Clark the keys. A very beautiful local woman in her late twenties. With very expensive clothes. Introduced as Maggie. She wanted the cottage as a quiet place to work out the options for her future. But what did she really do there?

'We picked up a rumour months ago in London that there were a bunch of Russians offering an assassination service for big money.'

Lenkov jumped in. 'Well, that couldn't be our lads. We would have known about it.'

'Yeah? Well, let's just check the facts. The police report states your two men – one from London and one from Warsaw – flew to Glasgow on the Wednesday and met with Clark. All false names. That's not in doubt.

'And their tickets were booked in London and paid for in cash. That's not in doubt either.

'Now these tickets are too steep for a two-day sight-seeing trip. Your London man organised this and paid cash because he was being paid cash to do a job. Probably by Clark acting for someone else.

'And we think the job was to bump someone off. We also think your London lad brought in a skilled killer from Warsaw. Sorry, Dmitri. To us, it's the only way it makes any sense.'

Dmitri grimaced. 'Okay, I accept what you say for the moment. On you go.'

'Right. So, we believe your men went out to the cottage in Rhu to kill someone. The car mileage in the police report matches two round trips from Glasgow.

'But it wasn't to kill the girl. She was there willingly and we believe she was part of the gang. We think she was there to lure someone else to that cottage. And we don't know who that is, or even if he turned up.

'So, we came to a conclusion last night. We don't think the Brits were behind this, because they would just have removed your men by car to a local prison.

'We think the Americans were behind it. They must have tracked your men for weeks or months for an offence somewhere. Then got Special Branch to help once they realised the men were in the UK.

'I'd bet that the Americans took your men out of the UK that night, and they now languish in prison in the US somewhere. But we can't prove it.

'And if you challenge Maxwell with this evidence from our report, the way we talked about, I think that's what she'll tell you.'

Dmitri glanced across the table. 'Vadim?'

He shook his head. 'Oh, I'll study your report and call her today as we agreed. But I'm shocked. I know we've asked all Russians to bring in more money where they can to get the economy working again, but I'd just no idea our people would do this.'

Paul turned to Dmitri. 'Are you happy with what we've done? Do you want me to dig deeper?'

'No, I'm happy with that. Paul. Good job. Let's see what happens on Monday and I'll call you if we need anything else followed up.'

'That's great.' He folded his papers into his case and stood. 'I'll arrange a final bill for you, but I'll be giving you some money back, I think.'

Dmitri stood. 'That's good. I'll walk out with you. Vadim, I'll be at Barclays later. Leave word with Jean on Maxwell's reaction.'

Lenkov stood and shook hands. 'Will do.'

Dmitri guided Paul out and they walked along Bayswater Road. 'Anything else on the other job?'

'Yeah, two points, Dmitri. Can we go into this café? I've got something to show you.'

They took a table at the back and ordered two teas. Paul pulled out another report. 'Two weeks ago, the woman Maxwell moved from the hotel into an apartment just south of Baker Street tube station, just north of Marylebone Village. The details are in my report.

'Last Saturday, a man moved in with her. Here's a photo of them last Tuesday. They look and act like a married couple, but she does not have a wedding ring.

'He looks American, and we've tracked him each morning to the American Embassy. He shows a pass to get in. So, he works there.'

'Do you have his name?'

'We don't, Dmitri. But, in a moment of inspiration, I sent this photo to my man in Glasgow and asked him to check it with his waiter witness. And we struck gold.

'The waiter said he noticed that woman at the hotel early on Thursday, July 11. The hotel manager drooled over her even more than usual. She had a sort of air of command about her. He'd asked a colleague about her. She was an Events Manager at a company in Glasgow. They could get a lot of business from her. So they were hiding her true ID.

'The waiter then said the woman met a man in the foyer and went walking down the driveway with him. Twenty minutes later, they arrived in the hotel lounge, where he was restocking the bar.

'His girlfriend served them tea and noticed they had an aerial photo of a boat at sea. The man left about twenty minutes later in a Royal Navy car. So he may have something to do with the Submarine Base at Faslane, three miles up the loch.

'The next time he saw the woman was in the Lomond Function Suite at a Silver Wedding buffet lunch. He was on servery duty.

'She had changed into a chauffeur uniform, which he thought was strange. She then disappeared, and he didn't see her again till late afternoon. Just after four.

'There had been all the excitement of the helicopter coming and going and now it was back for the fourth time. She strolled back up from the cottage area with the tall man in a flying suit.

'They stood close, like a couple, talking for a few minutes, before the man boarded the helicopter and it took off for the last time. And that man in the flying suit was this man in this picture with Maxwell.

'She came back into the hotel, changed clothes, and then left in a large car with two radio aerials. So she must have been very important.

'Putting it all together we think Maxwell and this man knew each other before the events of the day, and probably planned it. And they're now living together in London. Thought you'd like to know.'

Yeah, that's good, Paul. Thank you.'

'Do you want me to dig any deeper?'

'Let's leave it for now. See what happens Monday.'

'Okay, talk soon.'

They left the café, and Dmitri headed for the tube station. *That Maxwell woman had colluded with the American to grab the two Russian men seven weeks ago. Yet had written her report as though she knew nothing about it. Acting the little Miss Innocent. She'd given his aunt in Moscow so much grief. Wonder how she'd like a dose of her own medicine. Bloody bitch.*

Chapter 2. Sandra Maxwell

Sandra entered her boss's secretary's office two doors down in the Special Branch section of Scotland Yard. 'Is he free, Diane?'

'Just let me check for you, ma'am.' She buzzed through. 'CS Maxwell would like to see you, sir.'

'Send her in, please.'

Sandra knocked and entered his office. Dave Burnett looked up from behind his desk, smiled, and waved her to sit. 'Late Friday afternoon, Sandra? Must be crucial.'

'It is, sir. You know my report on the two Russians in Glasgow seven weeks ago?'

'Yes, of course.'

'Vadim Lenkov, the Chargé d'affaires at the Soviet Embassy here, just called me. Thanked me for the report, and asked if we were still willing to check further if they gave us more data.

'I said we would, and so they're coming in on Monday morning with it.'

'Do you know what it is?'

'Yeah, some of it. In my report, the two Russians met a local man in Glasgow, who used the false name, John Clark. We couldn't find his real name.

'Lenkov was under pressure because the younger Russian, Yushkov, based in Warsaw, has an uncle with links to the Kremlin. He shouted loudly about finding the two men.

'So they rechecked the office of the older London-based man, Golovkin, who seemed to be the leader in what they were doing, and found an unknown phone number in Scotland.

'They hired a firm of private detectives, who dug deep and found the false John Clark was a local lawyer named Norman Muir. Big step forward.

'The press reported him injured in a fight at a cottage in Rhu on Thursday, July 11, and flown to hospital in Glasgow in a USAAF helicopter at police request. But he died a few days later.

'The PDs went out to Rhu and found a witness who saw the helicopter airlift the man to hospital. He said it also did two other runs with men on stretchers. But the PDs couldn't find where it took them.

'Lenkov now believes the two other men were their Russian colleagues, and were airlifted somewhere else. They want us to have another look.'

'How close are they to the truth, Sandra?'

'They're there, sir. They know the USAAF airlifted three men, but can trace only one of them. In my view, to retain any trust, we should now direct them to the US Embassy. I suggest you warn Gary at the CIA that this is about to be blown open.'

'Okay. I'll call him now. And I'll join you with these Russians on Monday.'

'Thank you, sir. Just need to get our words right.'

***

'Hi, honey. I'm home.'

She looked up from her seat on the balcony as he stepped through the open double doors, leaned over and kissed her. He looked so good. Rugged, with that great smile. 'Scotch and soda?'

'Sure. Just gonna change. Back in a sec.'

Their first Friday night in London. They'd been apart for three weeks, during which she cleared her desk in Glasgow, and moved to London to take over as Head of Special Branch for London. A much bigger job.

She'd researched where to live, and decided on somewhere near Baker Street tube station. Only four stops from Trafalgar Square, close to where she worked.

Then refined it further to south of Marylebone Road, where she would then have a short walk north to the tube station and on to Regent's Park, or south to Marylebone Village, with its eclectic mix of shops and eating places, and on to Oxford Street.

She gave a property expert her spec. A top-floor furnished flat in that area, with a large sitting room and balcony facing west, two double bedrooms, (to allow for visitors), a good-sized kitchen and bathroom, in a well-maintained block with lift and porter services.

Within two days, he gave her his top three options. On one evening, she checked them, called Chuck to discuss her choice, and finalised the rental.

After two weeks in a hotel, she moved in and enjoyed her choice for a week before Chuck arrived from the US last weekend. He'd now left his USAAF service a year after the war ended, and trained for his new job as Head of Investigations for the CIA in Europe.

He came out on to the balcony, now dressed in sports shirt and slacks, and lifted his glass. 'Cheers. Real nice spot here. Good choice, honey.'

She lifted her gin and tonic. 'Cheers. Good week?'

He stretched his legs and leaned back with his face up to the warm evening sun. 'Yeah. It's been good. Bit different from running an airbase, though. But Gary's very good. Knows what he wants. It's a clean canvas and new structure, so we're kinda feeling our way. He wants us to join him and Sue for lunch on Sunday. Wants to meet you. I've already said yes.'

'Fine. I'd like to meet them too.'

'How about you? Good day?'

She grimaced. 'Good and bad.'

'Oh? What was good?'

'I don't know whether I've ever told you about my favourite phrase, "What gets measured gets managed." From Lord Kelvin. I applied it in Glasgow to measure our clear-up time for cases. There, we had broadly half cleared in a month, and the other half within three months. A few outliers didn't fit that pattern.

'But down here, the cases are more complex, and they didn't really measure it at all. So, we've taken the best part of three weeks for a small team to gather the data. And today, I got the summary.

'In broad terms, a third of cases, wholly within our control, get cleared in two months. Another third, that involve one other region, take up to four months. The last third, that involves two or more other regions, take up to six months. And if the Foreign Office is involved, it adds two months to any of these.

'There are also lots of outliers, better and worse, with no clear reasons why. We need to figure out how to work in parallel with other regions and the FO, and not just in series. It's a good start.'

'And what's the bad?'

'Did you see Gary before you left tonight?'

'No, I didn't.'

She told him about the phone call from Lenkov. 'Dave and I will see him on Monday. But we'll agree to re-investigate, and then find that you guys got valid extradition warrants on the two Russians from a Scottish court for the murder in Italy. So, it's all going to blow up for you next week.'

'Well, we knew it was going to happen sometime. It's maybe earlier than we expected.' He clapped his hands. 'Right. Where do we eat tonight?'

'How about going back to Marylebone Village? There's a great choice there.'

'Agreed. Let's do that.'

***

Sandra thought Sunday lunch went well at Wheeler's in Old Compton Street. Gary and Sue, in their early fifties, were great company, and seemed well matched.

'This is my favourite restaurant,' Gary said. 'Hope you like seafood. Best in London here.'

Sandra had the Dover sole. Incredible quality and flavour. Easily matched Gary's description.

The chat remained light and bright throughout. Sue was English and had married Gary eight years ago.

After lunch, when the girls went to the Powder Room, Sandra probed further.

'Where did you meet Gary?'

'At a mutual friend's party in '38. He worked at the US Embassy here, and I worked in advertising. We just clicked. It really was love at first sight. We were both recovering from messy divorces, and it was just right. And it's been like that ever since.'

'Oh, that's brilliant. Do you have a family?'

'Yeah. We've four kids between us. I have two daughters here. Both in the London area, and both with two children. So, plenty of grandkids to spoil.

'And Gary has two sons with families over in New Jersey. I think that's why he gets on so well with Chuck. They're both Jersey boys. Lived only twenty miles apart.

'Chuck comes from Ridgewood, a real nice village. And Gary from Boonton, a larger, more industrial town. The radio capital of the USA. It's where they make most of the radios in the US, including aircraft radios. Gary's sons work on these at ARC.'

'I look forward to visiting Ridgewood someday. I want to meet Chuck's daughter, Amy, and his brothers and their families. They sound a good bunch.'

'Oh, you'll love it over there, I'm sure. But just to help you in the meantime, I've got you a present.'

She went into her bag and brought out a small book, "Living and Working in America". 'This was a godsend to me when I went over in '39. I found living there more difficult than I expected at first. And their culture is very different. But I now feel more enriched and broadened from the last eight years. Use this guide. It will help you understand them.'

'Thank you so much, Sue. Very kind of you.'

'You're welcome. We better get back.'

As they stood on the pavement outside Wheeler's, Gary leaned forward, shook hands, and kissed Sandra's cheek. 'Great meeting you, Sandra. Hope to see you again soon. Just a word before I go. You and Dave are seeing these Reds tomorrow. And we'll pick up from you after that. But remember, they play by their rules, not ours. They have their own agenda in this fine world. Don't trust them.'

***

Sandra knocked on her boss's open door. 'That's the Russians here, sir.'

He rose from his desk. 'Okay. Let's go see them.'

As they walked downstairs, he said, 'Let's just listen. We'll re-investigate, but let's not discuss it.'

'Right, sir.'

They marched into the meeting room. Dave smiled and held out his hand. 'Good morning. I'm Commander Dave Burnett, Head of Special Branch. And this is CS Sandra Maxwell, who wrote the report to you when she was Head of West of Scotland region. She's now Head of London region.' They all shook hands.

'Yes, good morning. I'm Vadim Lenkov, Chargé d'affaires at our London Embassy. And this is Dmitri Bardin, a colleague from our Warsaw Embassy. Thank you for seeing us.' They exchanged cards.

Lenkov, tall and slim, with glasses, spoke good English, with a smile on his mouth but not in his eyes. Bardin, shorter and stockier, also with glasses, didn't smile. Just stared at her. Maybe he hadn't seen a woman in a senior position before. Lots of men around like that.

'I understand you want to discuss Sandra's report of July 15? How can we help?'

'Yes.' Lenkov looked straight at her. 'You state in this report that if we can provide more data on the missing men's plans and activities in the Glasgow area, then you would follow up and report back. Is that still the case, now that you are in London?'

She nodded. 'Of course. My successor in Glasgow, CS Malcolm Craig, will do that.'

'Good. We've been very active in the meantime. This is our private detectives' report. It gives their findings and the contact details of the witnesses if you need them. But they're now stuck,

'They know the first man airlifted to hospital was Norman Muir, the false John Clark. They also know our two Russian colleagues were with him that day, and were probably the other two men on stretchers airlifted that day as well.

'But our team cannot find where they were taken and don't know how to contact the relevant US military authorities. The nearest US airbase at Prestwick has now closed. And the local police in Helensburgh wouldn't or couldn't give them any further information.

'So, they've hit a blank wall. And we would like your help to find out what happened.'

Dave thumbed through the report. 'Okay, Sandra, would you send this to Malcolm in Glasgow, and ask him to re-investigate this case?' He stood. 'Thank you, gentlemen. We'll get back to you as soon as we can.'

Lenkov rose. 'Thank you. May I just remind you that our two colleagues had diplomatic immunity? Your police should have protected them.'

Sandra said, 'You'll see in my report that, under the Congress of Vienna, diplomatic immunity only applies to registered people on official duties in their real names. Their use of false names renders that invalid.'

'We beg to differ, ma'am. The Congress of Vienna says no such thing. If our people asked for immunity, they should have got it.'

Sandra shrugged. 'I'm sorry. I just don't agree.'

Dave stepped in. 'Thank you for coming. We'll get back to you with our findings.'

They escorted the Russians to the main entrance, and then went back to Dave's office.

'What do you think of that, Sandra?'

'I think they know more than they're saying, sir. Did you hear him? The contact details of the witnesses, if you need them? Nasty bastards.'

'Right. I'll brief the FO later. Let's get Malcolm on the phone. Did you brief him over the weekend?'

'No, I didn't, sir. Wanted to see what happened today. But I briefed him about it at our handover.'

The line connected. 'Malcolm. Remember the briefing Sandra gave you on the two Russians? Yeah, that's them. We've just had their bosses in here. They've had a bunch of private detectives on the case. Sandra will radio-telegraph their report. Can you re-investigate today, please? Re-interview their witnesses, and find out if they spoke to anyone else. Then get back to us later.'

***

Malcolm Craig called back later in the day. His team had met all the witnesses named in the PD's report, and confirmed their statements.

The only point of note was that the PD had asked the waiter at the Rhu hotel about the woman, Maggie, who had stayed at the cottage where the fight took place.

Sandra wondered why their report didn't mention this. But it meant Cathie, the lure, now well-hidden with a new ID in witness protection, could also be in danger. And that was a worry.

She then prepared her report.

'Further report by Special Branch, on request from the Soviet Embassy in London.

Background

On 02 September 1946, the Soviet Embassy asked us to revise our report, dated 15 July 1946, in the light of a report from their private detectives.

This gave us new data on the local man their two men met in Glasgow. Also of a fight in a cottage at Rhu on Thursday 11 July 1946. A US helicopter had airlifted this man and two others, who may be the missing men, to hospital after the fight.

But they could trace only the local man to the hospital. Not the two others. Hence this request.

Findings

Our team in Glasgow has now confirmed witness statements in the PDs' report, and has probed further.

On 11 July 1946, local police detained two men, one English, and one Polish, for the attempted murder of a UK citizen at Rhu. However, they were not charged, and therefore did not appear in police records at the time.

This was because US authorities had presented a prima facie case to a Scottish court that the two men had murdered a US citizen in Rome, Italy, on or around 12

June 1946. The judge granted their request to extradite these men for murder. This took priority over the attempted murder charge at Rhu.

US authorities invoked their warrants and removed the two men from the UK that day. They also sent copies to the men's home addresses from their ID documents, and to the relevant UK Embassies. For Smith, the British Home Office. For Kujawska, the Polish Embassy in London. The men carried no Russian ID.

The Soviet Embassy should now contact the US Embassy in London for further information.

Signed: Alexandra Maxwell, CS, SB London
Date: 02 September 1946'

She then sent her report, approved by Dave Burnett for the SB, and Vernon Hammond for the FO, to Lenkov at the Soviet Embassy. And to Gary West, Head of CIA Operations for Europe at the US Embassy.

Then waited for the fall-out to happen.

***

On Wednesday evening, Chuck told her the US Embassy had received a formal request from the Soviet Embassy in London to investigate her report. They had sent a holding reply saying they would get back to them as soon as possible.

She felt he wasn't his usual cheerful self. 'Anything wrong? You seem quite subdued tonight.'

'No, no. Everything's fine. Ten days into a new job. Usual doubts surface.'

'You want to talk about them?'

He grimaced. 'Don't know what to say. I suppose as an airline captain, I got tremendous personal satisfaction.

'Passengers and crew relied on me to get them to their destination safely. Earned huge respect.

'Much the same in the USAAF during the war. My teams relied on me to take the right decisions at the right time. And I think I earned huge respect again.

'But here, it's different. CIA is a new organisation. Kind of FBI for overseas. We're still finding our way. Still getting to know the team in Europe. And I can't see how to make an impact right now to earn that respect.'

'Okay. Can I give you a tip?'

'Sure. Of course.'

'You're in charge of investigations within Europe. So, you're the nearest thing to a cop within the CIA, right?' He nodded. 'Well, I think I'm more of a natural cop than you are. And I get huge personal satisfaction from delivering justice to victims of crime and putting crooks behind bars. And you've got to feel the same.

'With a new case, my brain kicks into solution mode to get the perps. Motive, means, opportunity? And get your measures in place like I talked about last week. Start with clear-up times. Can you do that?'

'Of course I can, honey. Really appreciate it.'

***

On Friday evening, they went to the pub they had visited last week, the Brown Cow in Marylebone Village. Tasty food, good beer, and a fantastic jazz band, whose toe-tapping version of 'Bill Bailey Won't You Please Come Home' brought the house down. They had to play it three times last week.

Tony, Assistant Manager, according to his badge, showed them to a table. 'Good to see you back, folks.'

When he'd gone, Sandra smiled. 'Do you think he really remembered us from last week?'

Chuck smiled. 'No chance. He probably says that to everyone. Makes them feel good.'

They ordered fish and chips and their beers, and enjoyed the music from the jazz band. The girl singer had a wonderful voice, and belted out the songs big style. The Bill Bailey number got the same rapturous reception as last week.

Chuck leaned over. 'Need the men's room, honey. Back in a minute.' He rose and made his way over to the bar area and toilets.

Sandra soaked up the atmosphere. The English pub, run well, was so much better than the somewhat dour Scottish pub. She enjoyed a great night out at this place. Packed with people having fun.

A few minutes later, she glanced at her watch. Nine o'clock. Chuck was taking his time. Must have met someone. But maybe she should just check.

She stopped a passing waitress. 'I need to go over to the toilets. Can we keep this table?'

'Yes, ma'am. One moment.' The girl went to her servery, came back with a RESERVED sign and put it on the table. She smiled. 'There you go.'

'Thank you.' Sandra headed for the toilets.

Outside the Gents, she looked around. Chuck would have come straight over here and then straight back. Where had he gone? Maybe he was still inside?

The lad, Tony, came towards her from the rear of the pub. She stopped him. 'Tony. Could you check whether my husband is still in the toilet, please? Six feet tall, grey sports jacket, blue sports shirt, dark slacks.' She used the word "husband" just to simplify matters.

He thought for a moment. 'Oh yeah. The American man? He was with you, right? When I came in from the garden area a few minutes ago, his mates were helping him out to get some air, they said.'

Her stomach churned. 'What? Show me where.'

'Sure.' He turned and pushed his way through the crowd and out a rear entrance into a wide garden area packed with tables and crowded with people.

She looked around. No sign of him. 'Is there an exit from here at the back?'

'Yeah.' He pushed his way through to an open gate at the rear that led on to an access lane.

She looked both ways. Empty. She turned, went into her handbag, and pulled out her warrant card. 'Tony, I'm a police officer, and I need to use your phone now. But first, tell me about these mates. How many were there, and can you describe them?'

'Yeah. Two. About the same height. Swarthy guys. Black sweaters and slacks, I think. Your man was kind of stumbling along. One mate on each side.'

'And when one said he needed air, did he have an accent at all?'

'Yeah. Now that you ask, he did have a strong accent. Not unusual around here, of course.'

'Okay. Take me to your office, please.' Her heart raced, but she tried to keep her head clear.

They pushed through the crowds again to his office. She picked up the phone and called nine-nine-nine. Let's get some boots on the ground here. Tony left her to it.

'Emergency. Which service please?'

'Police, please.'

A momentary delay. 'Police. How can I help?'

'This is CS Maxwell of Special Branch. I'm at the Brown Cow pub in Marylebone Village. Two men have just kidnapped my husband. He's a senior official at the US Embassy. I need officers here to find witnesses.'

'Right, ma'am. We're on our way.'

She called another number. 'Duty Inspector.'

'This is CS Sandra Maxwell. Who am I talking to?'

'Inspector Harry Davies, ma'am.'

'Harry. I need you to do several things for me now.'
She gave him a description of Chuck and told him what
happened. 'I think Russians may be behind this, Harry,
and they'll want to take him out of the country. We can't
allow that to happen. They're probably in a car now.
Maybe three big men and a driver? I want an alert out to
every port and airport, including private airports, to hold
these men with immediate effect.

'I'll get on to the US Embassy and get Chuck's
photo sent over to you. Can you circulate that as fast as
you can as part of the alert, please?'

'Will do, ma'am. How do I contact you?'

'I'll be here for a while yet. Then I'll come into the
office and see you.'

She then called Gary West, Chuck's boss at the US
Embassy, told him what happened, and asked him to
send Chuck's photo over to Harry Davies at SB.

Then six policemen arrived. She described what had
happened and asked them to question people around the
central bar area near the toilets, and in the rear garden
area to get a better description of the 'mates', and to get
any information on any vehicle in the access lane.

Then she phoned her boss and told him what had
happened. 'Bloody Russians, sir. Bunch of bastards.'

Chapter 3. Chuck Campbell

He woke and checked his watch. Nine o'clock. Didn't remember much. Packed Gents toilet with crowded urinals. Fastened his fly. Then a slight bump in his left thigh. Washed his hands. Feeling woozy. Two guys. One on each side. 'Need some fresh air, mate.' Out the door. Fresh air. Through the gate. Into a car. Big and black? Taxi? Need to tell her. Must tell her. Then nothing.

A light shone in the far corner of the room. White walls. Brown furniture. Bathroom over to his right. He rose slowly out of bed, staggered over, used it, and made it back to bed. Still felt woozy.

Was it nine the following morning or night? He couldn't tell. The room had no windows. A door in the wall opposite the bed. Steel tubes mounted to the wall on its right. A table and two chairs further over.

Two easy chairs, the on lamp and a bookcase to the left of the door. A wardrobe and set of drawers on the left wall. Bedside table and lamp to his left. A radiator on each side wall. Ventilator grills high up on each side of the door. Linoleum floor with several rugs. Ceiling not that high. Looked like a basement room. But where? No sounds. No hints.

Then the steel tubes moved into the room about two feet, with the wall now resealed. Mounted on wheels. He staggered over. A breakfast tray had arrived. Juice, tea, toast and cheese, and water. A note said, 'Leave Used Dishes and Any Requests Here in One Hour.' He tried to push the trolley back, but it wouldn't move.

He lifted the tray onto the table. The tea told him he was probably still in the UK. And the tray indicated breakfast time. So, around nine o'clock in the morning.

He finished breakfast, put the tray on the trolley, kept the small bottle of water, and relaxed in an easy chair. The bookcase had a selection of travel books, Agatha Christie novels, and a pad of paper with pencils.

He was still in his underwear, and got up, opened the wardrobe and found his outer clothes hanging, a robe and pyjamas on a shelf, and his shoes and socks, and a pair of light slippers, on a rack below.

In a bathroom cabinet, he found shaving equipment, toothbrush and paste, and soap powder to wash his underwear. Showed he'd be here for some time.

Gary had already talked how the Russians would want a prisoner swap. He just hadn't reckoned on him being part of it. Shit. Now what? And for how long?

***

At first, he thought the tapping noise was the radiator expanding or contracting. He had shaved and freshened up, realised he could do nothing about his position, so started 'The Murder of Roger Ackroyd'.

But the soft tapping became regular and insistent. Morse Code. SOS SOS.

He picked up a pencil and tapped a reply on the radiator pipe. SOS WHO ARE YOU.

The answer came, MAJ GREG JULICH USAFE 3 MARHAM UK.

Post-war, the USAAF had morphed into the USAFE, the US Air Forces in Europe. Chuck knew the 3rd Air Force had moved to Marham, Norfolk, and he had heard of a Major Greg Julich before.

The answer went on, HEARD THEM BRING YOU IN LAST NIGHT NEXT DOOR.

Chuck thought on balance, it seemed for real. Not a set-up. He tapped again. WHO ARE THEY.

MAY BE RUSSIAN. HEARD THEM TALK
WHEN LIFTED ME IN VILLAGE. WHO ARE YOU.

Chuck hesitated. Didn't want to give too much away at this stage. CHUCK CAMPBELL US EMBASSY.

COL CHUCK FROM PRESTWICK.

YES.

WOW DO YOU KNOW WHY.

PRISONER SWAP I THINK.

SO IT COULD TAKE A WHILE.

COULD DO.

ANY THOUGHTS OF ESCAPE.

ALWAYS BUT NEED TO KNOW MORE.

HAVE NOT SEEN ANYONE YET.

NOR ME.

OK KEEP IN TOUCH.

YEAH.

At least a fellow American next door. Lined up for a two-by-two swap. Options for escape? Close to zero. Didn't even know whether he was in a basement of an office block in a city or of a country house. Or even still in the UK. He picked up his book to clear his head.

**

Each day followed the same pattern. Breakfast arrived at eight. Lunch, tea and sandwich at one. Dinner, soup and stew, at six. Supper, tea and a small sandwich at ten. Each accompanied by a small bottle of water.

Chuck tracked the days. On day two, he requested fresh underwear, XL vest and L pants. They arrived next day with Marks & Spencer tags. So, he was in the UK.

By day four, he still had seen no one, but knew that Gary and Sandra would rescue him at some point. Fingers crossed. He picked up his book again.

Chapter 4. The Note

Over the weekend, Sandra tried to maintain a calm facade to hide her distress. She spent most of her time in the office going over her plans. But she had no leads.

Police officers at the Brown Cow on Friday night had picked up only vague notions of the "mates" who had helped Chuck out for "fresh air". None enhanced what she'd got from the lad Tony at the scene.

And the descriptions of a car were even hazier. Large and black. Though someone said they thought they saw a taxi in the alley.

Road blocks on the major routes from London threw up nothing. And nothing either from any port or airport. Chuck had gone, but she'd do her best to find him.

Gary West had come over on Saturday morning to meet with her and Dave Burnett to discuss how he could help. He'd already put his CIA teams in Europe on alert to pick up any leads.

Her SB group in London had five Divisions, Central, North West, North East, South East and South West. Each included several London boroughs.

On Sunday, she created her "war room" similar to one she'd set up in Glasgow. She would bring in leads on potential Russians from the London Police network, and manage them from there.

She pulled in Barry Crichton, the rising star from Central, who had done such a great job on her clear-up time analysis, to run it.

For each lead they would create a file and summary sheet with the date; from which Division, Borough and Officer; details of the suspect, with a photo if possible, and the reason for suspicion.

They would aim to verify the suspect's alibi for Friday 06 September at nine o'clock within five days.

They set up five rows of six boxes along the wall to contain the summary sheets. One row per Division, and each box covering Days One to Five and Five Plus.

First thing Monday, Sandra called a meeting of her five direct reports plus Barry. She brought them up to speed with events, and showed them the war room. 'Dig deep with friends, family and contacts in the Met. Find Russians. People who like vodka, caviar, communism, Russian literature and music. Get photos if you can. Check where they were last Friday at nine. And check taxi operators if they lifted anyone from the Brown Cow. Bit of a needle in a haystack, but let's try. We'll meet here twice a day to agree our actions on each lead.'

***

Dave Burnett had asked her to join his meeting at ten with Gary West from the CIA, and Vernon Hammond from the FO, to keep them up-to-date.

Ten minutes into the meeting, Burnett's secretary, Diane, knocked and entered the room, with an envelope. 'Excuse me, ma'am. The front desk sent this up for you. It's urgent.'

Sandra waved her to put the envelope on the table. 'Who delivered it?'

'A young boy ran in, gave it to the cop on the desk, shouted, "Pass it on", and ran out again.'

Sandra studied it. Addressed to her at Special Branch, with "VERY URGENT" in red.

She took a sheet of paper from her pad, folded it, then lifted the envelope inside it and looked at the reverse side. Nothing. 'Do you have a letter opener and some tweezers, sir?'

'I do.' Burnett got them from his desk.

She gently slit open the envelope. Then used the tweezers to pull out several sheets of folded paper. She laid them on the table and used the tweezers to unfold a typewritten note. 'Shall I read it?'

The others nodded.

She read aloud. 'This note is from Glorious Russia (GR). We are an unofficial group with links to Soviet Embassies in Western Europe.

'We know you sent a letter to Vadim Lenkov, Chief of the London Embassy, last week, telling him the US authorities removed our missing colleagues, Anatoly Golovkin and Sergei Yushkov, from the UK on 11 July 1946, using extradition warrants.

'This should not have happened. These men had diplomatic immunity, and you should have protected them. We believe the US authorities are now stalling us, and as a result, we have detained two US citizens in a secure location somewhere in Western Europe.

'They are Major Greg Julich of USAFE 3, Marham, and Mr Charles Campbell of the US Embassy, London.'

Gary slapped the table. 'Hell. They've got *two* of our boys. *Shit*.'

Sandra went on. 'We hereby notify you that if you return our two men to our Embassy in London by 17.00 hours on Friday, 13 September 1946, in time to catch the evening flight to Warsaw, then we will release your US citizens unharmed.

'However, if this does not happen, we will take action against them. You may know that Mr Yushkov lost the tip of his fourth finger on his right hand in an accident as a child. Our action will therefore cut off the tip of the same fingers on your Americans at 19.00 hours that evening. Not surgically, but by hammer and chisel. We will send the two cut-off tips to you so you can check their fingerprints.'

Burnett shook his head. 'Commie bastards.'

'We will then repeat the surgery every 24 hours on your men's other fingers and toes. You realise, I'm sure, your men would then lose their balance, could not use cutlery or play sports such as tennis or golf, and would never feel the smooth skin of a woman again.'

Sandra felt tears well up in her eyes, and slid the note along the table to Burnett.

'You can avoid all this. But, in the event we reach this point with our men still not returned, we would arouse their members to erection, and chop off the tip. If they lost this centre of pleasure, they would no longer enjoy being men.'

Sandra howled, sobbed, and dashed out to the ladies' room, into a cubicle, and vomited into the toilet bowl. 'Oh, God. Please don't let that happen.' She had never pleaded to any God ever before. And didn't know why she did it then.

She returned to the room ten minutes later. 'I'm sorry about that. Just couldn't help myself.'

Burnett nodded. 'Not a problem, Sandra. But don't let these bastards get to you. You've got to stay angry with them, and you'll come through it okay.'

'Thank you, sir.'

Gary cut in. 'And it won't happen anyway, Sandra. We always knew they would barter for their guys' freedom. It's just quicker than we expected.'

She felt she'd got over her trauma. 'Do you think Lenkov knows about this, sir?'

'Maybe. But he'll stick to the official line. He's a diplomat, after all. At the end of the note, they've asked us to put an entry in the Personal classified ads column of the *Times* tomorrow saying "GR. Agreed. SW." Gary will try to get clearance from the US, but we think we should go ahead with it.'

'What does SW stand for?'

'The Stupid West.'

She shook her head.

'You're right though, Sandra. Let's just check with Lenkov.' He asked Diane to get him on the phone.

'Morning, Commander. What can I do for you?'

'Well, it's not a good morning for us, Mr Lenkov. May I tell you first you're on a speaker phone at this end? With me I have Sandra Maxwell, Mr Vernon Hammond from our Foreign Office, and Mr Gary West, Head of US CIA Operations for Western Europe. Have you heard of a group called Glorious Russia?'

'I have not, Commander. I don't know who or what you're talking about.'

'We've just received a letter from them. May I read it to you?'

'Of course. Go ahead.'

Burnett read out the letter. Sandra's stomach turned again, but she controlled it this time.

'I'm sorry, Commander. I know nothing about this.'

'Well, it's clearly from someone who has seen Sandra's report to you. How widely was it issued?'

'We sent it to the relevant senior managers at our London and Warsaw Embassies, and our Ministry HQ in Moscow. But I haven't heard of this group before.'

'Do you support them?'

'Well, I support their aims if not their means. That's horrific. But we do think our men had immunity. You should not have allowed the Americans to take them. We have written to the US Embassy as you suggested, but they're stalling us.'

'Can I point out they don't have immunity from committing murder elsewhere in Europe?'

'We doubt that's true.'

'What? Even though the US authorities won these warrants in a Scottish court of law?'

'Well, it was a one-sided case, and we believe they rigged the evidence. We don't accept it.'

'So, does that mean you won't do anything about this group and their gruesome proposals?'

'Not at all. I'll try to find out who they are and what we can do about them. But I don't promise anything. I'll need to think where to start. Goodbye.'

Burnett hung up. 'Sorry, Gary. Did my best.'

'You sure did, Dave. Don't be sorry. It's up to us now. And we know a lot more about where we stand.'

***

On Monday afternoon, Dave Burnett visited her war room. She walked him through the process, and showed him a couple of leads that had already trickled in.

He nodded. Good job, Sandra. Just what we need.'

'Thanks, sir. Hope we find that one lead.'

'I've just had Gary West on the phone. He's tried to find out about Greg Julich, the other American. There was no flag raised because he's on a four-day weekend pass. Planned to spend it with a woman in London.

'The Marham airbase had a team investigate what happened. He hitched a ride in a Jeep on Friday morning into the village. Had something to pick up at a bespoke jeweller. Then get a cab to Downham Market to catch a train to London for a great weekend.

'The jeweller said he bought a special brooch for his girl. Really cheerful. Then left to walk to the taxi company a hundred yards away.

'The taxi company owner says he never arrived there. So the team then checked the other businesses along the main street.

'The greengrocer saw a man dressed like him talking to a passenger in a taxi outside his shop around eleven. The man then got into the taxi and it drove off. He described it as an ordinary London taxicab, but didn't note the reg number.

'The only other point is that the airbase had a call from a woman around two o'clock asking for Major Julich. He had arranged to meet her at the National Gallery at one, but hadn't turned up.

'The operator couldn't contact him, and gave the standard reply that operational staff could have their schedules changed at short notice. She took a note of her name and number.

'The team called her today. A feisty Irish woman called Ann Quinn. Very peed off that Greg hadn't turned up and hadn't called her. The team assured her it wasn't his fault, and they'd get back to her.

'So, Gary's assuming Julich was picked up by the Russians on Friday morning in a London taxicab in Marham village. And that's what we should work with.'

'Wow. These Russians are sly bastards, sir. But expert at what they do. Might be hard to catch. Let's hope our war room does the trick.'

Chapter 5. Dmitri

On Monday afternoon, Dmitri rang the doorbell at Paul Lynch's home. A large terrace house just up from Holland Park station. Nice area, he thought.

Paul opened the door. 'Dmitri. Come in. Come in. Good to see you. When I called Jill this morning, she told me you were still over here. And this is just perfect. Would you like some tea?' They walked through to an office overlooking the rear garden.

'No, thanks. I'm fine. Just had lunch. You've got something for me, I believe?'

'I do, Dmitri. Since we met last Tuesday, my man in Glasgow has put in a lot of work to help you understand what happened up there in July, and he and I have talked about it over the weekend. But you won't be any less angry than you were last week.'

'Angry? I was bloody livid. They were so dismissive last Monday. Then their report I gave you on Tuesday? Extradition for murder? No Russian ID? Just don't believe it. And they act like they didn't know about it? Gave us the runaround. Treated us like shit.'

'Well, that's typical Brits for you. Anyway, let's turn to what we've found. We've got two bits of info for you. One of which we think is pretty solid, and one which is more speculative. But together, they show what happened to your men was a major piece of work by the Brits and Americans, well planned in advance.'

'Okay, tell me.'

'When you gave us the go-ahead on Tuesday, my man in Glasgow went back through his notes to find out where to start. He discovered a comment by his waiter witness that he'd never followed up.

'This related to the first helicopter landing when the tall man in the flying suit got out. Once the engine noise stopped, the waiter realised there was a commotion at the entrance to the access road to the cottages.

'An ambulance had arrived with its bell ringing, but couldn't get through the barriers because there was a large black car trying to get out. So, who was trying to get out from the cottages as the ambulance was going in?

'To cut a long story short, my man found the driver of the ambulance, who told him the large black car had two men in the rear seat. And as the ambulance squeezed past, the man on that side looked up.

'He was a big man, very well dressed, dark suit, white shirt and striped tie, with a florid face and silver hair. Quite distinguished looking.

'So, where had he come from, and why had he visited that remote cottage? My man did some more digging and found there had been a big celebration at Faslane that morning. It's only three miles up the loch from Rhu. And the *Glasgow Herald* carried a photo of the VIPs attending.

'He got a copy of the photo, took it to the ambulance man, and he identified the man in the car. A hundred per cent. He's Sir Anthony Hewlett-Burke, the Chairman of two large industrial corporations in the UK.'

'Really? And why was he at the cottage?'

'Well, we've talked about it. And the best reason we've come up with is that the beautiful Maggie lured him there. We think he was the target.'

'And what about Maggie? What happened to her?'

'We don't know. We're pretty confident she was part of the gang. The rentals woman said she was a pleasant local girl when she looked round the cottage. So, if that's the case, the police would arrest her too.

'But my man has checked every court in Scotland for the three weeks following that day at the cottage, and she doesn't appear anywhere.

'So, we think that, for whatever reason, this girl blew the whistle on the gang, including your men, and she's now in a witness protection programme. That's why the police could plan it all so carefully, and pull the target out before the gang moved in.'

'Wow. So what do we do now?'

'Good question, Dmitri. What do you want to do?'

'What about this man, Sir Anthony? What do we know about him?'

'We've tracked him since last Thursday. He lives on his own in a big house on the outskirts of Birmingham near the head office of his companies.

'Divorced last year. Ex-wife now in Southampton. Son and family in Birmingham. Daughter and family near Southampton.

'Spent Thursday at head office. Friday, got early train to London office. Left at two-thirty, went to Foyles bookshop, then at three-thirty to Victoria's Tearoom next door, where he had a reserved table. Probably goes there every week. Then at four-thirty a taxi to Euston and train back home.

'Weekend largely spent at local country club. Tennis on Saturday morning. Golf on Sunday morning. Dance on Saturday night. No particular female companion.

'Here's my report to date, with photos and details. Do you want us to continue tracking him?'

'Yeah. Keep it going to the end of the week. Let's build up a picture of him. Don't know how I'd use it, though. If what you say is true, and he was the target, then someone somewhere wanted him dead, and paid big money for it. And that's a big decision. How could we find that person?'

'He's a big businessman, Dmitri. Must have made lots of enemies along the way. Sounds like a needle in a haystack job.'

'Well, is it? I'm in business too. And you're right. I've made a few enemies. But business enemies get back at you via business. For someone to want to kill you takes it to a different level. A personal level.

'And the other question I ask is, why Glasgow? Where are his main business activities?'

'According to official records, he has multiple facilities in Birmingham, Manchester and London, but they service the whole of the UK from there, though it's mainly England.'

'Right. So, let's assume he personally slighted a business contact in a big way in Birmingham. What would that contact do to take revenge? To kill him.'

'Probably check his local contacts to see if they knew someone to do it.'

'Exactly right. And in this case, the local man was in Glasgow. So I'd suggest you start there and see if you can find a local businessman so slighted by Sir Anthony that he arranged for his local contact, Muir, to organise his killing. What do you think?'

Paul nodded. 'Yeah. That's good. We'll do that.'

'And what about the girl, Maggie? She's the only member of the gang left. And you said she was local as well. Maybe she would know the paymaster? And if she blew the whistle on our men, I'd like to grab her. How could we find her?'

'Well, if she's in witness protection, it would be damned difficult. The prosecution service would organise it, and she could be anywhere, with a new ID. But I suppose we could try.'

'Good man, Paul. Here's another bunch of fivers. Keep digging.'

Paul wrote him out a receipt. 'How long are you here for, Dmitri?'

I'm probably going back next week, but I've got other business interests here, so I'll be back over every two or three weeks. I'll keep in touch. *Udachi*.'

***

Dmitri left Paul's house and headed for the tube station. On the way, he stopped at a phone box and called Jill Graham. 'Hi, Jill. It's me. Anything for me?'

'I have, Dee. Mr Lenkov wants you to call him. Says it's urgent.'

'Okay, I'll do that. Anything else?'

'No, that's it. See you later.'

'Should be with you by six as usual. Where is it we're going tonight, again?'

'A local pub, with a slot for experimental theatre. For my friend in the theatre group. So it's really just to give her some support. If it's too way out, we can leave and get back to the flat.'

'Oh, I remember now. No problem. Bye.'

'Bye.'

He hung up. The arrangement with Jill worked well for them both. They enjoyed each other's company, and the sex was good. She knew he had a wife and family in Moscow, and made it clear she was happy with a casual relationship with him in London.

Most nights, he stayed overnight with her, and kept a change of clothes and shaving kit there. He rented an office at Barclays International when he needed it, but also had a room and office at the Nash Terrace house that he visited twice a day. His staff there knew better than to ask where he stayed overnight.

He picked up the phone and called Lenkov. 'You wanted me to call urgently?'

'I did, Dmitri. Have you heard of an organisation called Glorious Russia?'

'No. Never heard of them. What do they do?'

'Well, we think they may be an unofficial group within the Soviet Embassy network that maybe our man Golovkin and your Sergei were part of.'

'What makes you think that?'

'I've just had Commander Burnett on the phone. He's had a letter from this group, addressed to Sandra Maxwell, saying they've detained two Americans at a secure location in Western Europe.

'If she delivers our two men to our Embassy by five o'clock on Friday, to catch the evening plane to Warsaw, the Americans will be freed. If not, they'll be tortured.'

'Bloody hell. Do you know who's behind it?'

'We don't. Though we suspect some senior people that were close pals of Golovkin. But they all deny it.'

'Well, they would, wouldn't they?'

'Yeah. There was some criticism of our response last week. Some said we were too soft just requesting the men's return. We should have been much harder.'

'Well, it's a point of view.'

'Yes, but international diplomacy works by taking the right small steps that everyone understands.'

'Right. Make that clear to them.'

'We're doing that.'

'Good. What are the next steps, then?'

'They asked her to put an agreement in the Personal column of the *Times* tomorrow. So we'll see what happens then.'

'Fine. Can you keep me in the picture?'

'Yes, indeed.'

'Okay, talk again soon.' Dmitri hung up and smiled. His strategy was now in place and running.

Chapter 6. Lorna

Six weeks after arriving, Lorna Mitchell was bored with Spain. It had been a mistake to come. She could've gone anywhere. But had been attracted by an advert for Sunny Spain. Now, in September, the plush Miramar Hotel in Malaga had become like a deluxe prison. She couldn't walk out of the hotel grounds without someone who spoke good Spanish. And the city wasn't great. She just didn't enjoy her new life here.

As usual, she was a magnet for men. But apart from Alex, whom she had met on her first morning, they were all sleazebags. Either British or Spanish. She stretched out on her sunbed and thought about her future.

She wanted to get back to London. But first needed to talk over her options with her Swiss banker and lover, Armin. He had set up all her finances in Malaga, and would give her the best advice for moving to London. Then she would talk it over with Lynn, her contact in Glasgow, who'd arranged her new ID, and brought her to Spain.

Ten minutes later, a shadow came over her. She looked up, shielding her eyes. A man knelt down and spoke quietly. 'Miss Mitchell, I'm Carlos Pereira, the hotel manager. I request you come to my office please. We have the police visit. They want to talk with you.'

Lorna sat up. Her tummy leaped. Police? *Shit*. She had spent so much of her life bending and stretching the law. She didn't like the police. 'Can you tell me why?'

'I can't. They just want to talk to you.'

'Okay.' She stood, slipped on her sunglasses, kaftan, high-heeled sandals, and wide-brimmed sunhat, and went with the manager to his office.

Her heart raced, but she tried to stay poised. She marched in. Two men stood as she entered. Both very Spanish in white shirts and ties. The older with a heavy moustache. The younger clean shaven. She held out her hand. 'Buenos dias. I'm Lorna Mitchell.'

They shook hands. The manager left and the younger man spoke. 'Miss Mitchell, this is Inspector Massana, and I'm Officer Ruiz. We'd like to speak to you about a man named Alex Jardine, whom we think you know. Or at least you've spent time with here.'

She sat and felt relieved. 'Okay. Happy to help.'

'How well do you know Mr Jardine?'

'Not well, really. I met him six weeks ago when I first arrived here.'

The inspector asked a question in Spanish. Ruiz translated. 'Did you know him before you came here?'

'No. We're both from Glasgow, Scotland. He heard my accent.' Ruiz translated back. 'He's been very kind. Took me to various cafes and restaurants. Showed me some landmarks around Malaga.'

'Are you here on holiday?'

'Yes. Kind of. My father died recently and left me a small legacy.' *Stick as close to the truth as you can, girl.* 'I came here for a few weeks to sort out my future.'

'So, was it a holiday romance with Mr Jardine?'

'No, no. We just enjoyed each other's company. But there was no romance. He's married with a family back in Glasgow.'

'I see. Were you with him last night?'

'Yeah. We had dinner together. Then he went off to a business meeting. I joined a group of Brits in the bar. We meet most nights after dinner.'

'And were you there for the rest of the night?'

'I was. Played cards – solo whist – with three others. A couple called Keith and Sarah, and a man called Bill. We played until the band packed up about eleven.'

'And then what?'

'Had a final nightcap then up to my room.'

'And so you were in your room by when?'

'About quarter to twelve.'

'What time did Mr Jardine leave you?'

'About half-past nine.'

'And he was going to a business meeting?'

'That's what he said.'

'Do you know what his business was?'

'He imported special pills from Germany. Sold them through pharmacies along the coast. Branded them "Vivo" for men and "Viva" for women. He said they were widely used in Germany. But unknown over here.'

'What's so special about them?'

'He told me they make you feel bright, lively, and active. Help you forget your worries.'

'Did you ever try any of these pills?'

'No. Never. Would you mind telling me why you're asking these questions?'

'At midnight last night, Mr Jardine was found dead. Floating in the water at Playa La Caleta, about five hundred metres east of here.'

'Oh, my God.' She put her hand to her mouth.

'On the face of it, he drowned while swimming. His clothes were on the beach. But we're treating it as a suspicious death for the moment. Did you ever know him to go for a midnight swim in the sea?'

'No. Not even a midnight swim in the pool here. And he was a good swimmer too.'

'Really? That's interesting. Coming back to his business. Do you know how he sold these pills along the coast? Did he do it himself?'

'I don't think so. His Spanish was not that fluent. I think he used local people to sell and deliver. He met locals at the hotel here from time to time.'

'Could you describe them?'

'Sorry. I couldn't. They were just local men. Though I saw him talk to a local woman at times. Pretty, about twenty, nice smile, long hair a sort of ponytail.'

'That's helpful. Were you ever in his room here?'

'No. Never.'

'Oh. That's a pity. The maid said there were lots of boxes in his second bedroom. But they're no longer there. I just wondered if you ever saw them.'

'I'm sorry. I didn't.'

'Well. Not to worry. You've been very helpful.'

She stood and shook hands with them. 'You're welcome. Am I now free to go?'

'Yes. We're talking to all the Brits. To build up a picture of where you all were last night.'

She left the room and headed back to the sun terrace. *Should maybe think about moving out sooner rather than later*. She didn't know how well her new ID would stand up to scrutiny by the local police. Better call Armin this morning. Get the process started.

***

She took a taxi to the Head Office of the Banco de Santander in the city centre, and asked for the manager, Mr Laborda. When she had come in six weeks ago to activate her account, he had been all over her like a rash.

She reckoned Armin must have put a VIP flag on the account to get such a reaction. Or maybe he just did that all the time. He came towards her, arms outstretched, with a big smile. 'Miss Mitchell. Delighted to see you again. And looking so good. Come in to the office.'

She had dressed the part. A pale grey short-sleeved business suit with white blouse, matching bag, shoes and hat, and sunglasses. All top of the range from the hotel shop. She'd had her hair styled on Friday, and liked her soft tan. 'Thank you very much.' She entered his office, and he sat behind his desk.

'What can I do for you this morning, ma'am?'

'Four things. I want to lift some cash. Get some travellers' cheques. Arrange travel to London. And make some international phone calls.'

'Ah. You're leaving us so soon?'

'Just for a couple of weeks. I have some business to attend to in London.'

'Good. I'll get Blanca, our International Manager, to help you.' He lifted the phone and spoke in Spanish.

A few minutes later, a woman in her thirties entered the office. Looked very capable. 'Blanca. This is Miss Mitchell.' The girls shook hands.

'Let's go up to my office and get you organised.'

Lorna stood and shook hands with Laborda. 'Thank you for your help. Much appreciated.'

'Our pleasure, ma'am. Have a safe journey.'

Blanca guided her upstairs to her office. 'Let's get your travel arranged first. We do this regularly for our British clients. When do you want to leave?'

'Tomorrow morning, if that's okay?'

'Yes. Tuesday shouldn't be a problem. Is it first-class all the way? It's much better and not much more expensive. I'd advise it. And do you want facing or back to the engine?'

'Face the engine, please.'

'I'll call the travel agent. Can I have your passport?' She picked up the phone and spoke in Spanish for several minutes, taking notes. She hung up. 'Right, that's it arranged. They'll have the tickets and itinerary over here in about an hour.'

'That's great.'

'So, your train for Barcelona leaves at nine. You have a booked seat, and lunch is included.

'A man will meet you off the train. He'll have a board with your name on it. Take you to a top-class hotel. You're booked in for dinner, bed and breakfast.

'On Wednesday, the man will take you from the hotel to the station. Your train to Paris leaves at nine. It's the same deal. Booked seat and lunch. And a man will meet you in Paris, and take you across the city to a hotel near the Gare du Nord.

'On Thursday, the man will take you to the station and see you on the train to Calais. You then just follow the crowd through Customs on to the ferry across the Channel. You'll have access to the first-class lounge and lunch on board.

'At Dover, again follow the crowd to the train for London. You have a booked seat, and should arrive in London mid-afternoon. That's it.'

'Brilliant. Thank you.' It sounded a lot better than her journey from Glasgow, which seemed endless at the time, and took almost five days. Money talks.

'Okay. So, let's get your phone calls arranged.' She stood and opened a door in the wall behind her desk. 'You can use this office. It's very private. Now, what's the first number you want?'

Lorna checked her notebook, wrote Armin's name and Zurich number on a pad, and passed it to Blanca

She picked up the phone and spoke in Spanish. Then hung up. 'Takes five to ten minutes to connect. I'll leave you to it. When you want your next number, just knock on my door.' She left the room.

Lorna sat and thought about what she would say. Then the phone rang. She picked up. 'Hello?'

'Hello, my darling girl. Good to hear from you. How's sunny Spain?'

'Oh, Armin. It's just great to talk to you again. And Spain is sunny and … boring.'

He chuckled. 'Well, I warned you.'

66

'I know. But it's been a good break for me. And I'm coming back to London. Should be there by Thursday. Are any of your flats free at all?'

'Well, you can have your old flat back if you want. Same deal as before.'

'What? That's fantastic.'

'Yeah, the girl the agents found to replace you turned out erratic and disruptive. Didn't pay the rent and had raucous parties. Moving her out as we speak. We'll have the place spick and span for you on Thursday.'

'Brilliant, Armin. Really appreciate that.'

'No problem, darling. And I'll be visiting London every month. So look forward to getting together then.'

'Oh, I look forward to that too. Special times, huh?'

'Yes indeed. I'll give you the name and number of the chap at the agents. Have you got a pad?'

'I have. Go ahead.' She noted the info.

'Call him when you get there, and he'll come round, clear the paperwork, and give you the keys. Look forward to seeing you soon.'

'Can't wait, Armin. Thanks so much.'

'You're welcome, darling girl.'

She hung up and thought of him. Almost ten years since they met. Just after she moved to London. At a banker's dinner, where she was a hostess. And they just clicked. He was such a skilled lover, and they satisfied each other so much. She relished their time together. Okay, so he had a wife and family elsewhere, but it was still an idyllic life for her. Love to get it back.

But now for her other option. With the only man who'd fallen for her ability as well as her beauty.

He'd made it clear in June that she had made a big impact on him three years earlier, during the war, when she'd arranged and run a War Office meeting for key suppliers at which Churchill spoke.

Now divorced, he wanted her as his escort at business functions, and maybe more. Though only if she was interested. She checked her notebook and wrote his name and Birmingham phone number on the pad. Then went and knocked Blanca's door.

She came in and smiled. 'Another number?'

'Yes. In Birmingham. He knows me as Maggie.'

She didn't turn a hair. Not the first time she'd heard an alternate name. She spoke to the operator again and left her to it.

A few minutes later, the phone rang. 'Hello?'

'Maggie?'

'Yes, Tony. It's me.'

'Wow. It's been so long. I just assumed this wasn't going to happen.'

'I've been abroad.'

'Oh. I see.'

'But I'll be back in London on Thursday. Do you still have your Friday afternoon tea next door to Foyles?'

'I do.'

'Would you like me to join you?'

'I'd love that, since our last meeting was so rudely interrupted. But can you do that? I thought you had to break all ties with your past life.'

'Well, we didn't have any ties. One casual meeting and a ten-minute set-up? I don't call them ties.'

'Okay. If you're happy about it, I'd love to see you on Friday, Maggie.'

'Good. I'm now called Lorna, by the way.'

'Fine, Lorna. See you Friday. Bye'

She hung up and smiled. *Didn't know how that would go. But it was worth checking out.*

Then she asked for a third number. Lynn Blackburn, her witness protection contact in Glasgow. She ought to tell her she was coming back to London.

'Hello? Could I speak to Lynn, please?'

'She's not here at the moment. Who's calling?'

'Lorna Mitchell.'

'Can I give her a message?'

'Ask her to call me this afternoon.'

'Okay. Will do. Bye.'

She knocked on Blanca's door, and joined her. 'That's me finished. Thank you very much.'

'Good. And you want cash and travellers' cheques? What are you looking for?'

'Just for minor spends in Barcelona and Paris. To buy something that maybe catches my eye. Do you have the cheques in British pounds?'

'Yes, we do.'

'Okay. For cash, one hundred pesetas and one thousand French francs. And two two-pound cheques.'

'No problem. I'll get that for you. Excuse me.' She left the room for a few minutes and came back with the cash and cheques. 'Here you are, and the travel agent has just delivered your tickets.' She passed them over.

Lorna checked the details. Just as Blanca had said earlier. 'Thank you so much, Blanca. You've been very helpful. How much do I have in my account?'

She checked her notes. 'You have three hundred and twenty-seven pesetas, ma'am.'

'When I come back, I may go down to Marbella. I assume you have a branch there?'

'We do. Part of our region. So there's no problem with using that branch.'

'Good. So, I'll get on my way. How much do I owe you for all this?'

She did a quick calculation. 'That's a total of two thousand three hundred and sixty-three pesetas, including the phone calls, ma'am.'

'I'll give you a cheque on my Swiss bank,'

'No problem, ma'am.'

Lorna wrote out a cheque. Every time she did this, Armin's words came back to her. '*You've got twenty-six thousand in the account now. You're a very rich woman.*' Okay, half of it was her brother's. But she still always felt good writing a cheque. She passed it over. Then gathered her papers into her handbag, and Blanca showed her out. 'Thank you so much, Blanca.'

'You're welcome, ma'am. Have a safe trip.'

Lorna got into a taxi and asked for the rail station. She checked where to go in the morning.

Then she went to the adjacent bus station and approached the Information booth. 'Buenos dias. Do you speak English?' she asked the woman.

'Yes. A little.'

'Tomorrow? When do buses leave for Marbella?'

'Every hour from seven am to ten pm.'

'Thank you.'

'Do you want a ticket?'

She thought for a moment. Her brother told her always to make her cover story real. To live it. And she didn't want the local police to know she was leaving the country. 'Yes, please. For the nine o'clock bus.'

'Ticket for any bus.'

'Okay. How much?'

'Six pesetas, ma'am.'

She paid the woman and put the ticket in her purse. 'Thank you.'

'You're welcome. Bus from platform four.'

She left the building and took a taxi to the hotel. Her favourite receptionist stood behind the desk. 'Buenos dias, Miguel.'

'Ah. Senorita Mitchell. How are you today?'

'I'm good. Could you make up a final bill, please? I'll be leaving tomorrow morning.'

'Oh, no. I don't want you to leave. You're my favourite British guest.'

'Well, it's only for a few weeks. Just a bit upset by the news of Mr Jardine. And the other Brits will talk about nothing else for days now. So I'm going to Marbella to get away from it all for a while.'

'I quite understand. I know you were close to Mr Jardine. He was a fine man. A great loss. But I heard the Inspector tell our Manager that all the British guests were now in the clear. They're looking at his business contacts. So, I hope that helps you.'

'It does, Miguel. Thank you.'

'Can we organise a hotel, or a car to take you to Marbella tomorrow?'

'No, no. I visited there last week. There are a couple of new hotels opened at the far end of the village. I'll get into one of these, I'm sure. And I feel almost local. I've already got my bus ticket.' She lifted it from her purse.

'Good for you, ma'am.'

'But can I leave a second suitcase here tomorrow? Then once I've chosen my hotel, I'll call and you can send it on to me?'

'We'll do that with pleasure, ma'am. I'll leave a note for the desk staff tomorrow.'

'Thank you, Miguel.'

'You're welcome, ma'am. And we hope to see you again sometime soon.'

She left the desk and went up to her room to change. Then threw herself on the bed and thought about what she'd done. And it all felt good.

***

On Tuesday morning, she took a taxi to the bus station, walked through to the rail station, and presented her ticket at the gate. Once through, a uniformed porter picked up her suitcase and showed her to her seat.

There were six seats in the compartment. A couple from Paris in the two seats at the corridor side. And a well-dressed English woman in her forties opposite her at the window side. Her name was Alice.

They mostly just read their books as the train wound its way along the Spanish coast. She and Alice took the first sitting for lunch, and the Paris couple the second to keep the compartment occupied.

In Barcelona, Alice had the same hotel, and so they hired an English-speaking tour guide for an hour who showed them the sights of the city. The unique Sagrada Familia, the wonderful Placa d'Espanya, and a stop for a drink on Las Ramblas to people watch. Lorna admired the Spanish women and their colourful outfits.

Wednesday was pretty much a repeat, with a tour of Paris to see the iconic Eiffel Tower and Notre Dame, and a stop at Montparnasse. She thought the women in Paris showed great chic from the cut of their clothes and the way they walked. Much greater than in London.

Lorna enjoyed Alice's company. But in true British fashion of strangers meeting, they chatted more about what was going on around them, than about themselves.

When she said goodbye at Victoria Station on Thursday afternoon, the only things Lorna knew about Alice were she lived in Belgravia, had "a place" near Marbella, had a husband who was "something" in the City, and had two daughters at boarding school who were on holiday with a cousin in France. A whiff of wealth and elegance. But they would never meet again.

Of Lorna, Alice knew even less.

She arrived at the block of flats in South Kensington and called the letting agent. Her name was already up on the board against Flat 3. Within minutes, she had signed the papers, got the keys, entered her flat, and flopped into her easy chair. Home, after nine weeks away.

Ten minutes later, she gave herself a shake. She had to get food, drink and household things before the shops shut. She still had British money in her purse and her Ration Book somewhere in her handbag.

She made a list of what she needed and went out and bought the lot. Once she had put them away, she went across the hall to her neighbour's door and rang the bell.

The maid, Betsy, answered the door. Her face lit up with a big smile. 'Ma'am, it's you. Are you back?'

Lorna smiled. 'Yes, I'm back. Will you let Tamsin know, please? And if she has a few minutes to spare in the next hour, can she pop over and say hello?'

'Oh, she'll be ever so pleased you're back, ma'am. She's really missed you. I'll tell her.'

'Thanks, Betsy.'

She went back to her flat and poured a gin and tonic. Twenty minutes later, her doorbell rang. It was Tamsin.

'My God, Greta, you look fantastic. Where have you been?' She came into the hall and hugged her. Lorna closed the door. 'I've only got a few minutes till my next man arrives. But can we meet on Monday as usual? I want to hear all about it.'

'Yes, of course.'

'Oh, that's great.' She heard her doorbell ring. 'I need to go. That's him arrived. Here for his half-hour of heaven, dressed in his padded bra and satin blouse. Easily pleased. See you on Monday, Greta.'

'By the way, Tamsin, I'm now called Lorna.'

'Lorna? That's nice. Okay, see you Monday.'

She closed the door. Life back to normal again.

***

On Friday afternoon, she entered the tearoom next to Foyles at three-thirty, and approached his table in the far corner. She had brought back her best British clothes, and wore her grey suit and shoes, white sweater, dressed much the same as when they had first met there.

He watched her approach. A smile of approval spread across his face. He stood, shook hands and kissed her cheek. 'Wow. You're more beautiful than ever, Lorna. Where have you been?'

She sat and smiled. 'In Spain, Tony. Relaxing in the sun for the last few weeks.'

'Why did you come back?'

'It just wasn't for me.' *Let's butter him up a bit.* 'But also to see you again. You're unique in my life.'

'Really? In what way?'

The waitress served the afternoon tea, and Lorna selected a sandwich. 'Because you're the only man who ever admired me for my ability to run a meeting, and not just for my looks.'

He chuckled. 'Yeah. It was a magical moment to meet you again by chance in the bookshop. Though it wasn't by chance. Was it?'

She dropped her eyes. 'No, it wasn't.'

'So, who asked you to do it?'

'The man who organised the hit. John Clark.'

'And why did you agree?'

'Because he blackmailed me into doing it.'

'On what?'

'He had evidence that would put me away for five years if it fell into the hands of the police.'

'Genuine?'

She thought for a moment. *Stick to the truth. See where it takes you, girl. He probably knows anyway.* 'Yeah. On a previous hit.'

'Was that the one your brother was jailed for?'

His detectives had done a good job. 'Yeah.'

'So, tell me what happened at the cottage after I was whisked away by that detective.'

'When you were out the front, the police switched on the light at the back of the house. That was my signal for the gang to move in. After they entered the house, the police emerged from the bedrooms and arrested them. Cuffed and gagged them.

'But then one of the Russians kicked out at Clark and knocked him into the fireplace. Smashed his head. They airlifted him to hospital, but he died.'

'Oh, too bad. Do you know who was behind it?'

Dangerous territory. Act dumb. 'No. And I don't think Clark knew either.'

'Yeah, well, I think I know. So, why did you blow the whistle on this job?'

'Didn't like Clark. He wasn't good enough. And I hated the killers. The Russians. Also, to get out from under the blackmail and cut a deal with the police.'

'Did you do that before you knew I was the target?'

'Yes. At that point, I only had a photo of you. But I didn't know your name. Clark wanted our bookshop meeting to be as natural as possible.'

'It certainly was that.' There was a long silence as he halved a scone, layered it with cream and jam, and took a bite. 'On the way home, I savoured that meeting. Even thought about being together, with you at my side at official receptions and dinners. Perhaps even marriage. But then the doubts crept in.'

'What were they?'

'Two things, my dear. When I told you I knew who you were, I saw a flicker of fear in your eyes. Only for a millisecond. But it was enough to make me wonder if there was an ulterior motive.

'And then to find out you would be in a remote cottage near Faslane on the same days I was there, was too much. That's when I asked the man behind you to check up on you.'

She turned and realised the man behind her at the next table was Snuff, his personal security man. She'd focused so much on Tony, she had missed that.

'Did your man, Clark, have an inside contact at Faslane. Is that how he knew my travel plans?'

'That's correct.'

'Yeah. I knew it had to be something like that.' He took a cake from the stand. 'The question is, what do we do now? Where do we go from here?'

She sat with bated breath as he ate his cake.

'You're a remarkable young lady. Since you called on Monday, I've wrestled with that question.'

'Does it matter what I think?'

'Fair point. What do you think?'

She took a big breath. 'I could easily have stayed in Spain. New name. Anonymous. The British men I met were probably all on the run from the law here. The British women spent their divorce money on sunshine, booze and young Spanish men. Just not for me.

'You told me you'd throw your hat in the ring for me if the occasion arose. So that's why I came back. To see if that was still true.

'I've changed my life. No more crime. I now want stability. Certainty. To feel wanted for what I really am capable of. Hence why I'm here.'

He finished his tea. 'You know, I could so easily love you. I don't think I've ever desired a woman more. You're beautiful, clever, and indeed capable. I'd love to just grasp your hand and take you home with me.'

Let's hope there's no buts, she thought.

'But.' *Shit, there is.* 'I have a rule in business that's served me well over the years. Don't let your heart rule your head without a reality check.

'I pay Snuff lots for my reality checks. He tells me I should avoid you. Says you're too much baggage. Too much of a risk to my reputation.

'Now, I don't always agree with him. But, in this case, I'm afraid I do. And so, it ends here, my dear. With a heavy heart, I'm walking away.'

She grimaced and looked straight into his eyes. 'I'm sorry to hear that, Tony. Is that just for now? Or if I'm a good girl for say a year, would you reconsider?'

'I stick with my decisions, Lorna. I don't think so.'

'Ah well, it was worth a try.'

'Yes, it was. A tough choice. I hope you find what you're looking for, my dear.' He glanced at his watch. 'But I now need to catch my train home.'

He waved to the waitress, paid the bill for both tables, and stood. 'Do you want Snuff to see you home?'

'No. I'm fine, thanks.'

She watched them leave the tearoom and catch a taxi. *Shit.* Hadn't worked out for her. Now what? Her mind was numb.

A few minutes later, she left, walked down the road to the tube station, and caught a train home. As she walked to her block of flats, she realised she hadn't done her usual "last on last off" routine. Well, it didn't matter. No one from her past life knew she was back.

Chapter 7. Black Friday

Sandra arrived in her office early as usual, and set her desk calendar. Friday, the thirteenth of September. *Oh, shit.* As a child, she had picked up her mother's habit of always taking extra care on such a day. Because it was unlucky. And today was the day she'd get Chuck back. Fingers crossed.

There had been a huge row earlier in the week. Gary had put an "agree" response in the *Times*. Even though his boss had shouted "their two guys for our two guys".

Lenkov pointed out he didn't know this GR group. So he couldn't act as a go-between. Gary had to decide for himself what he'd do.

She went to her war room. Barry was updating the leads. She knew the pattern. A trickle to start. Peak within a few days. Then back to a trickle. And only remove leads with alibis for both kidnaps.

Her team assembled at nine, and Barry walked them through a summary. 'As of now, we have thirty-seven leads, of which we've got rid of fifteen.

'This is day five for the Monday leads, and all three have gone. So that's good.

'Of the six leads from Tuesday, we still have two left. So we should focus on them today. Both from Central. Brian has the details.'

'Thanks, Barry.' He checked his notes. 'Both these leads came from cops' wives. Both focus on Russians called Dmitri. Seems to be a common name. And we expect to discard both as well. We just can't confirm their alibis yet. That's the hold-up. Do you want to hear any more details?'

Sandra nodded. 'Yeah. Let's hear about them.'

'Right. The first, lead four. From the wife of a Met cop. She'd bought a set of Russian dolls from a shop in Petticoat Lane. It had loads of Russian antiques. And the owner was Russian. Been over here twenty years.

'Our team saw him on Tuesday. Dmitri Krayev. Here's his photo. Mid fifties. Slow moving. Widower. Lives by himself. Was in his shop on Friday morning and at home Friday night. But we can't confirm the latter. Says if we want to talk to Russians, there's a club every Sunday in Camden Town. Though I doubt they'd inform on each other. But this man just didn't do it.'

She studied the photo. 'Yeah. Doesn't sound like it.'

'The second, lead eight. From the wife of one of our cops. She's a member of a theatre group. Makes the costumes. Last weekend, as she finished one off for a show on Monday, her sewing machine jammed.

'She called a friend she works beside, who lives nearby, and who let her use her sewing machine. But it ran out of thread.

'She went through to the other room to find more thread. Her friend got it from her sewing box in the sideboard. With the door open, she saw two bottles with fancy foreign labels, and asked what they were. Her friend laughed and said they were high-class vodka that Dee, her boyfriend, brought over from Moscow.

'After she finished the costume, they sat and chatted for a while, and enjoyed tots of the vodka.

'The friend's name is Jill Graham, and our team talked to her on Wednesday at Barclays, where she works. Her boyfriend is Dmitri Petrov, known as Dee. A high-flying businessman from Russia who makes regular trips over here.

'We saw him on Wednesday evening at her flat. He's a banker. Invests in very bright people, with clever ideas and a passion for success. Finds them in top universities, such as Oxford, Cambridge, and London.

'Last Friday, he caught a train to Cambridge about ten. Had lunch with Professor James Cawthorne. They then went to a nearby lab and met with a young man called William Pryce. He'd conceived a new barium based oxide to make magnetic tape. He wanted new funding to take it to the next stage.

'Petrov was impressed, and agreed a contract for the next twelve months. Later, they all went to a local pub to celebrate. They parted around five.

'Petrov loves Cambridge, and spent the next few hours around the town. Trinity College. King's College Chapel. And the Mathematical Bridge among others.

'He grabbed a bite in a local café and caught a train around seven-thirty that got him into Kings Cross around nine. He got back to her flat just before ten.

'The girl confirms he was in her flat when she left just after eight in the morning, and returned just before ten at night. Professor Cawthorne confirms he was with him from around twelve to five. The rest we can't verify at this time.

'His train tickets were clipped but not time-stamped. He came across as open and honest. On balance, we think he's clear.'

'So why do you hesitate, Brian?'

He grimaced. 'I'd just like to be more confident on the trains he took to and from Cambridge, ma'am.'

'I had a case a few years ago, Brian, where we had to prove a suspect didn't travel on a given train.

'A railway exec told us ticket clipping was like a signature. The clippers had different shapes, and every ticket inspector clipped the tickets his own unique way.

'We got them to check our suspect's ticket, and they proved he had travelled on a different train. We never tested this in court because, when we challenged the suspect with this evidence, he changed his plea to guilty. You should check whether it's the same here.'

'I like that, ma'am. We've got photos of his tickets.'

'Have you got a photo of the man?'

'Yes. Here it is, ma'am.'

She studied it. All these Russians looked the same. Square-faced with high cheek-bones. Similar to the lad from Warsaw she'd met ten days ago. At the time, she asked Gary to have his team in Warsaw check the ID of Dmitri Bardin, and they'd confirmed he worked there.

She handed the photo back. 'Okay, thanks, Brian. Can we do a quick run-through of the others, Barry? You all happy with that?'

They all nodded. She now hoped to get around fifty leads in total, with the crucial one somewhere within it. Fingers crossed.

***

Sandra had a sandwich lunch with her boss, Dave Burnett, to bring him up to date with her case. But getting Chuck back had taken over her thoughts. She just couldn't relax until the swap had completed.

Gary called just before two. 'Hi, folks. Just to let you know the two Russians are now here. We flew them in overnight. I'm about to call Lenkov and deliver them about three. Are there any points you want to make?'

Burnett glanced over at her, and she shrugged. 'I've got Sandra here. She wants Chuck back on a personal level, of course. But we see it as your show, Gary.'

'Yeah. You're right.'

'Are you still having problems with DC?'

'Ah, you wouldn't believe it, Dave. You think you have trouble with Westminster? You ain't seen nothin' like DC. Full of politicos driven by self-image. Most of them have hardly been out of their home state, far less the US. They see world politics like a Western movie.

We're the cowboys. The Russians are the Indians. And they all want to play Tom Mix.'

Burnett chuckled. 'How do you deal with that?'

'I've told them this bunch of Reds are like renegade Indians who don't play by the rules. But they still want to go in with all guns blazing. I try to stay calm in the middle of it all.'

'Well, good luck. I think, to answer your question, these Russians won't want to expose themselves. So they'll just drop your lads somewhere local. It would be good if it was near a police station. But you've just got to wait and see what happens.'

'Yeah. You're right, Dave. I'll just deliver them as planned. Talk to you later.' He rang off.

Burnett shook his head. 'He's struggling. Let's hope it goes okay.'

***

Dmitri called Lenkov just after two. 'Any news on what's happening with our two men, Vadim?'

'Yeah. Just had Gary West on the phone. He's the lead American. Will deliver our two men at three. Still demanding we have his two men available for swap. I've told him yet again we can't help him. We don't know where they are.'

'You still don't know who's behind it?'

'We don't, Dmitri. Though we suspect it's one or more of Golovkin's security people.'

'Right. Sounds the most likely. Can I come over and see our Sergei?'

'Of course. You can see both of them if you like. They ought to thank you for what you've done. We'd never have achieved this so quickly on our own.'

'Thanks, Vadim. See you later.'

He arrived at the Embassy just after three, and found the two men in the centre of a small crowd. Feted and treated like heroes. He asked Lenkov, 'Can I talk to Sergei on his own, please?'

'Sure. Use the room over there. I'll get him for you.' Lenkov separated Sergei from the crowd, and brought him to the side room. He then left and closed the door.

Sergei was his usual sullen self. 'What are you doing here? Didn't expect to see you.'

'Thanks. It's good to see you too. Your exploits left your mum sick with worry. So my dad asked me to get private detectives to find out where you'd gone. And then to speed your freedom. But some of your pals seem to have stepped in to make it even faster.'

Sergei shrugged. 'We knew it would happen.'

'Oh, did you? So, what about your mother? I suggest you phone her. Let her know you're safe.'

'Yeah. Okay.'

Dmitri picked up the phone and asked the operator to get the number in Moscow.

'It'll take ten minutes. So, we know a girl lured a target to a cottage for you to kill. But what happened there? How did the Americans get you?'

'Yeah. Seemed a good idea at the time. But that bloody bitch, Maggie, must have ratted on us. When we went in the back, we saw her out front with the target. We reckoned she'd be back in a minute. But then the police jumped us. They must have hidden in the other rooms. They cuffed and gagged us. Knocked us out. Next thing we were in America.'

'Why didn't you carry Russian ID?'

'That was Anatoly's idea. We did all these jobs with false IDs to hide our tracks.'

'I'm told the Americans got you for the murder of an American in Rome. Is that true?'

Sergei shrugged. 'No comment.'

'That means it *is* true.' *Shit*. The phone rang. Dmitri picked up and passed it to Sergei. 'It's your mum.'

'Hi, mama. It's me. Yeah, I'm safe. In London. In America. Back in a few days. Thanks. See you.'

'Right, one more call. To my dad. And you better thank *him* for what he's done.'

A few minutes later, the phone rang. Dmitri said, 'Hi dad. Got someone here wants to talk to you.' He passed over the phone.

'Hello, Uncle Oleg. Thanks for your help in getting me back. Yeah, I'm fine. Next week. Okay, thanks.' He passed the phone back to Dmitri.

'Yes, dad.'

'Are they coming out tonight?'

'Yeah. We've lined up security. Flying to Warsaw tonight. Then on home. They'll go to the Ministry first.'

'Right. When are you back?'

'Got to finish a couple of things here. Next week.'

'Good job, Dmitri. See you then. *Udachi*.'

'Thanks, dad.'

***

Sandra sat at her desk and stared out the window. But saw nothing. So worried about Chuck. She glanced at her watch for the hundredth time. Five o'clock. Still no word. *Shit*. How long will this torture go on? She couldn't sleep at night. Couldn't think during the day. Knew she wasn't on top form. But hoped it would end today. There was a knock on the door.

'Come in.'

Brian, her number two, popped his head in. 'Still here, ma'am? Can I have a word?'

'Sure. Waiting for a call.' She waved him to sit.

'Just had a call from the railway company. They're keen to help, but it might take a week or more.

'They have over twenty ticket inspectors based at Cambridge, and almost two hundred at King's Cross. And seven different designs of clipper. So there are lots of the same clipper around the crews. And they don't know which inspector has which clipper design. So they need to find that first.

'The other problem is they use large crews of inspectors on peak-hour trains, and small crews on off-peak trains. So the crews can vary from eight on peak trains to one on off-peak. But they do track the crew roster for every train.

'The problem arises because an in-bound train to King's Cross in the morning will be packed and require a large crew roster, but the returning train to Cambridge will have few people and require a small crew roster. And of course, the reverse in the evening. So most of the large roster on the packed train will not be on the roster for the returning empty train.

'But in practice, it doesn't work that way. Some of the non-rostered inspectors on the empty train will also check tickets to help their rostered colleague complete his tasks more quickly and have more time to relax.

'So, once they find which inspectors have which clippers, they then need to find out which trains the non-rostered ones travelled back on last Friday. And then work out which trains our suspect could have travelled on, and which he couldn't.'

'Bloody hell. Can see how it would take a week. But it'll be worth it to get a definitive answer.'

'That's right, ma'am. The other thing I wanted to check is what we talked about this morning. Going to the Russian Club on Sunday. What do you think?'

'I think your comment was right, Brian. They won't tell us anything. And I don't want to show my hand like that. Just forget it.'

'I agree, ma'am.'

Her phone rang. She grabbed it. 'Hello?'

'We've got the manager of the Adelphi Hotel wants to speak to you, ma'am. Shall we put him through?'

Her heart leaped. 'Yes, please.'

'Is that CS Sandra Maxwell?'

'It is.'

'I'm John Warner, manager of the Adelphi Hotel in the Strand. We've just found a man lying in our underground car park, with a bag tied around his head, and an envelope in his top pocket addressed to you. He's carrying a US driving licence in the name Gregory Julich. What do you want us to do?'

'Is he conscious?'

'Yes, but he's pretty groggy. Looks drugged.'

'Hold on a sec.' She covered the mouthpiece. 'Brian, can you get a car to the Adelphi Hotel in the Strand? They've found Greg Julich in their car park. I'll get them to check whether Chuck's there too.' Brian dashed out.

'Right, Mr Warner. I'll have a car with you in a few minutes to bring Mr Julich here. I'd like you to do two things for me, please.

'Could you recheck your car park for another man in a similar situation? There may be two men involved in this. And could you find out how the man got there? And please keep this matter confidential.'

'Okay, ma'am. I'll do that now.'

She hung up. Her heart raced. Her head now clear. She rang her boss, Dave Burnett, and then Gary West at the US Embassy. 'I'll be right over,' he said.

Brian came back into the room. 'The car's on its way. Should be back in ten minutes. Is Chuck there?'

'They're checking. Do we have a doctor here?'

'Yeah. There's always one on call.'

'Could you get him up here, Brian? Let's get Julich checked out.' He dashed out of the room again.

Sandra paced the floor, hoping Chuck was there too. But she'd need to find out from Julich where he'd been. Get any clues she could from him, groggy or not. She asked an officer to bring in pots of tea and coffee.

Ten minutes later, two officers helped carry Julich into her room and seat him at her conference table. Mid-thirties? Tanned. Handsome. Dressed in sports shirt, light jacket and slacks. 'No other man there, ma'am.'

'Okay, thanks.' Sandra introduced herself, her boss, and Brian. 'Would you like tea or coffee, Greg?'

He tried to hold his head up. 'Coffee, please.'

She poured him a cup. 'Milk? Sugar?'

He shook his head, held the cup in two hands, and sipped it. Gary arrived and introduced himself.

Then the doctor arrived and checked Greg out. 'I'm going to take a blood sample. See what they gave you.' He went through the procedure. 'He's on the way to full recovery. But just take it easy for the rest of the day.'

Greg put his jacket back on. Sandra sat beside him. The others spread around the table. She noticed the envelope in his top pocket. 'Is that for me?'

He nodded. 'Think so.'

She pulled it out. Addressed to her at Scotland Yard. She extracted a typewritten paper, and read it aloud.

'This note is from Glorious Russia (GR) again. You're annoying us. Stop looking for us. We have broken none of your laws. Just borrowed your men for a valid purpose. Put an ad in the Personal column of the *Times* on Monday saying "GR. Agreed Stop. SW." and we release Campbell.'

Burnett snorted. 'Other than bloody kidnapping.'

Sandra thought for a moment. 'Must be someone we've already talked to, or close to someone we've talked to. And that's only a few people.'

Gary grimaced. 'From our point of view, Sandra, we'd rather have Chuck back than catch these guys.'

Burnett nodded. 'I agree with that, Sandra. Pause your campaign until we get Chuck back.'

'Okay, sir. Brian, could you pass the word on to the others, please?' She turned to Greg, still slowly sipping his coffee. 'Greg, are you able to tell us how they got you and where they've held you for the past week?'

He glanced up at her and closed his eyes. 'Yeah. It was in Marham village. I'd just bought a brooch for my girl.' He felt in his pocket and pulled out a small box. 'Still got it. My girl. I need to call her.'

Gary leaned over. 'We'll call her later, Greg.'

'Okay. I walked along the main street, and a London taxicab pulled up at my side. The passenger asked me if I could tell him the way to the airbase. He had an urgent package to deliver and had taken a wrong turn.

'I gave them directions, and he asked if I was going somewhere myself. I said I was going to catch a taxi to the station. Going to London. He said if I guided him to the airbase, he would take me to the station for free.

'Sounded a good deal, so I got in and guided them towards the airbase. I think he bumped my leg as we turned a corner. But I remember nothing else until I woke up in a basement somewhere.'

'Can you describe this passenger?'

'Yeah. Maybe my age? Well dressed. Dark suit. Blue tie with a matching cloth in his top pocket. Dark hair. Glasses. Heavy moustache.'

'Did he speak with an accent?'

'Don't think so. Sounded English to me, ma'am.'

'What about the driver?'

'Didn't really see him. Dark hair. Flat cap. Checked jacket. Typical taxi driver.'

'And what about the basement? Anything unusual? Train sounds? Aircraft? Traffic noise?'

'It was very quiet. Think it was out in the country somewhere. Bedroom and bathroom. Food good. Colonel Chuck Campbell in the next door room.'

'How did you know that, Greg?'

'We spoke by Morse Code on the radiator pipes. He reckoned they held us for a swap.'

'Did you see anyone else?'

'No one. In fact, now you ask, they delivered food by an unusual kind of trolley arrangement. They could push a small section of wall into the bedroom carrying a tray with food and drink, and the wall then resealed.

'We had an hour to eat the food and put the tray with the empties back on the trolley. They then pulled the trolley back to the other side of the wall, and it became sealed again. Only they could move the trolley in or out.'

'And what happened today?'

'They must have put something in the food at lunch. It knocked me out this afternoon. Don't remember a thing till I woke up at the hotel.'

'Okay, Greg. Thanks for that.' She turned to the others. 'Gary? You take it from here?'

'Sure, Sandra. Come on Greg. Let's get you over to the Embassy. Make your phone calls. Let you recover there. Then back to the airbase tomorrow?'

Within minutes, everyone had left except Dave Burnett. 'Diane's working on tonight. I'll get her to organise the ad for Monday. I know you're disappointed about Chuck, but let's do what's necessary to get him back. Try to relax, and get some sleep.'

'Thank you, sir. Is it that obvious?'

'Yeah. You're doing well. But it's taking a toll.'

'Okay, sir. I'll do my best.'

'Good. See you Monday.' He left the room.

Her phone rang. 'Mr Warner, ma'am.'

'Hello, Mr Warner. What do you have?'

'We've spoken to our car park gateman at length, ma'am, and we think a taxi dumped your man here around ten to five. Hotel guests found him about twenty minutes later.'

'Did he take a note of the taxi's number?'

'He didn't, ma'am. He only notes the names and car numbers of guests parking overnight. The taxi driver was just delivering an urgent package, and couldn't get a space at the front. Hence why he came round the back.

'But there was no package delivered to Reception. So we think he just dropped the man off. In and out in two minutes, ma'am. Described as just a typical taxi driver. Had a gabardine coat and flat cap.'

'Thanks, Mr Warner. Appreciate your help.'

Typical taxi driver? They were the same words Greg used. Was this taxi significant? They'd got nowhere checking the taxi companies for anyone at the Brown Cow. Did someone own a taxi privately? It was such an anonymous vehicle. You never really noticed them. Was someone hiding in plain sight?

She just felt tired and thought about Dave's words. He was right. She needed to get back in full control. Try to switch off over the weekend. Get some fresh air and exercise. Get some sleep.

Chapter 8. Blue Monday

First thing Monday, after Jill left for the office, Dmitri strolled to the shop on the corner and bought a *Times* newspaper. He checked it back at the flat. The message was there. That would get Maxwell off his back for a while, and he would release Campbell later today.

The visit of two cops to the flat last Wednesday had thrown him. Just checking on the movements of Russian people the previous Friday. Wouldn't say why. But he bloody knew why.

He'd forced himself into a friendly, open posture with them. Nothing to hide. Spent the day at Cambridge. Evidence the train tickets from his expenses claim.

Then they took photos of the tickets. *Shit*. Could they tell which train he'd used? Don't think so. And they'd taken a photo of him. Couldn't refuse. Lucky he had changed his hairstyle and wore glasses for the meeting with Maxwell a couple of weeks ago. Would she see the photo? Would she make a link?

Now need to think about moving out sooner rather than later. And leaving no trail. Anywhere. He took a damp cloth and wiped every hard surface he had touched in the flat. Just to be sure. Repeated it every day.

Just after nine, the phone rang. It was Jill. 'Oh, good. You're still there, Dee. Would you call Paul Lynch, please? He says it's urgent.'

'Yeah. I'm just leaving now. I'll do that.'

He left the flat, dumped the *Times*, and called Lynch from a phone box. 'You wanted me?'

'Yeah. Are you free to come over? I've got something I think you'll like.'

'What is it?'

'Pictures of the girl, Maggie.'

'Great. Be over in half an hour.'

Lynch showed him into the office. 'Remember you asked me to track Sir Anthony up to Friday?'

'Yeah. Of course'

'Well, he visits a teashop next to Foyles on Friday afternoons. And last Friday a girl joined him. Very attractive. Late twenties. Light tan.

'After an hour, he left her to catch his train home. She looked upset. Got the feeling that whatever she'd asked for, he'd refused. Also got some pictures of her leaving the teashop,'

Dmitri studied the photos. 'Quite a stunner, huh?'

'Yeah. Sure is. But these two knew each other. And I wondered if she was the girl, Maggie, from the cottage. So I radio-telegraphed the photos to my man in Glasgow and asked him to check.

'He went out to Rhu, met the woman who fixed the rental, and she confirmed, a hundred percent, this girl rented the cottage for the two nights in July.'

'Wow. Good work, Paul.'

'Thanks, Dmitri. We tailed her from the teashop to a block of luxury flats in South Kensington. We've had it under obs for the weekend, but she hasn't appeared. And there's no Maggie on the name board in the lobby. So we don't know her present name. And that fits with her being in a witness protection programme.'

'Luxury flat in Kensington? How the hell can a girl like her afford that? WP wouldn't pay for it.'

'Good point, Dmitri. And I think we might have an answer for you on that one. Do you want us to keep going with this?'

'No. You've done your job, Paul. And a good one. But there's no further action needed. We got our men back on Friday. Job done. I'm going home this week.'

'What? How did that happen?'

'Well, let's just say Lenkov, or someone close to him, made the Americans an offer they couldn't refuse. No further details.'

'You'll be pleased, then?'

'Yeah, I'm glad it's over. Thanks for your help, Paul. We couldn't have done it without you.'

'I've typed up a report for you. It also includes my last item for you.'

'What's that?'

'You thought a local man must have funded this hit at the cottage. I asked my Glasgow lad if he could link any local businessman with a contract killing within the last two years.

'He asked around, and one of his network told him of a businessman in Ayr, just south of Glasgow, who had been attacked on his yacht by three men a year ago.

'The official police line stated the attack happened during the failed theft of his yacht. But the word on the street says it was an attempted contract killing. The man only survived because a US helicopter rescued him. How about that? Spent months in rehab. Now a recluse. But rich enough to pay for this hit.

'However, we can't connect these two businessmen. They work in different areas. The cottage man has two large engineering businesses. The Ayr man owns a store. There's no obvious link. Except one.'

'What's that?'

'Hold on to your hat, Dmitri. The girl.'

'What? The girl Maggie?'

'Right. Or, as she was known then, Jean Munro.'

'Bloody hell.'

'My man in Glasgow showed his pal the photos of the girl when they talked about the contract killing. The pal confirmed, a hundred percent, she was the girl he thought was part of the gang. But she skipped town before the attack, and the police couldn't prove it.

'The three of us talked about it yesterday. We think this girl is an expert lure, used by gangs all over the country, to bring rich men to a remote location so the gang can rob or kill them. And she's good at it. Likely earns a lot from it. And that's why she can afford a luxury flat in Kensington.'

'Wow. Take me over to it, and we'll call it quits. We can settle up.'

'I've done that, Dmitri. I owe you ten back.'

'Keep it, Paul. Treat your wife on me.'

'Thanks very much, Dmitri.'

'Yeah. You did a good job on this one.'

Paul drove him over to South Kensington, showed him the block of flats, withdrew his team, and left him to it. 'Hope to see you again, sometime.'

'Thanks for your help. Bye.'

Dmitri stood under a tree and watched the entrance to the flats. He pulled out the photos of the girl and studied them. This was the girl who had betrayed Sergei and his mate. Caused all this upset for his family. Told the police. Maybe even rewarded by them. She deserved to pay a price for that deceit.

He went into a nearby phone box and called Igor, his UK business manager. 'I'm at South Kensington. At the junction of Pelham Street and Pelham Place. Come in the taxi, and bring one of these special syringes.'

***

Sandra held her morning meeting at nine as usual. Felt refreshed after the weekend. She'd forced herself out of her flat both days.

On Saturday, she went to nearby Regent's Park, strolled around the boating lake, had lunch in a café, and enjoyed a brass band concert. On Sunday, to London Zoo for the day.

She'd learned London was a great city with Chuck, but a large and lonely place without him. Hope this Russian gang would release him today.

'Right, lads. You all got the message on Friday that we paused the search for Russians?' They nodded. 'Well, let me explain what that means.

'We only pause contact with Russians. But we keep our internal work going, and any other external contacts.

'For me, three things came out of Friday. First, the note from the Russian gang left with Major Greg Julich. They told us to stop looking for them.

'That means, within the thirty-seven leads we had on that wall on Friday, we've already talked to a gang member. Or someone close to them.

'Now, we'd already got rid of fifteen. But we may have to check them again for contacts. So, could you each review these fifteen again, please?

'Second, Julich mentioned a trolley structure used in his basement room to provide food.' She described it. 'The room wall was sealed whether the trolley was in or out the room. So they must have done it for a purpose and it took building work to install.

'We need to find it. He thought he was in a large house in the country. But I'm sure London also has quiet areas. Do you know which property agents would handle top end houses like this?'

Brian said, 'I think we start with Savills, ma'am. They're probably the biggest. Then check others.'

'Okay. Call them, Brian. See if anyone recalls a property with this type of trolley structure in it.'

'Will do, ma'am.'

'Third. Julich says a guy in an ordinary London taxi lifted him in Marham village. And the Adelphi Hotel thinks a taxi dropped him off in their car park. Barry, could you check whether people can buy a London cab, and use it as a car?

'Taxis are highly regulated, and so there may be a record if anyone does this.'

'Will do, ma'am.'

'Good. So, we put our response in the *Times* this morning. Let's hope we get Chuck back today. Thanks, lads. Let's keep going on this.'

***

Lorna couldn't believe it. For the first time in her life, a man she'd set out to attract had rejected her. The one man who'd admired her skills in running a meeting as well as her beauty. He wanted to throw his hat in the ring if she became free, he'd said. Left to himself, he'd have gone with her. But his security man, Snuff, had turned him against her.

From his remarks at the cottage, Snuff knew her real name. And knew her brother, one of his best men during the war, had landed in prison. His team had unpicked the maze of false names she had created to protect herself. *Shit*. But he'd also said, "The boss really likes you." So, something must have changed. Or maybe the man just took cold feet when he saw her again.

When she'd arrived back at her flat on Friday, she'd stripped off, put on her nightie and dressing gown for comfort, poured a large gin and tonic, and flopped into her easy chair to answer the question, "What now?".

Now, on Monday morning, still in the same clothes, with more gin than food, she stared at her image in the mirror. She still had no answer.

Come on, girl. Give yourself a shake. It's not the end of the world. You've come through problems before. Get yourself back in the game. You'll see neighbour Tamsin tonight. She always gives you a laugh with stories of her fetish clients. Come on, go for it.

She showered, restyled her hair, applied make-up, dressed in a comfy frock, had a decent brunch, and made a list of what she needed at the shops.

Also some exercise and fresh air. So planned to walk up to Hyde Park, and stroll round the Serpentine before doing her shopping. *Right, let's get on with it.*

She left her flat, enjoyed the warm sunshine, passed the tube station with hordes of tourists flocking towards the V&A Museum, and waited to cross the busy Cromwell Road.

People pressed in all around her, and she felt herself collapse. Someone screamed, and a man shouted, 'Let me through. I'm a doctor.' He opened her eye and lifted her wrist. 'This girl needs a hospital. Taxi! Taxi!' He lifted her into the taxi and shouted, 'Driver! Take us to the nearest hospital. Fast as you can, please. *Udachi.*' Then she blacked out.

***

Late morning, Sandra looked up at a knock on her open door. Brian asked, 'Got a minute, ma'am?'

'Sure.' She waved him to a seat.

'Just talked with a Senior Partner at Savills. He says ten years ago, when he ran the Regent's Park area, he sold two Nash Terrace houses with that trolley system in the basement rooms.

'He'll dig out the files if we want to go over at two o'clock. Do you want to come too, ma'am?'

'Sure. Sounds a great lead.'

'He's at Lincoln's Inn, so we should leave here about a quarter to.'

'Good. Well done. Look forward to it.'

Ten minutes later, Barry arrived. 'Got some info on the taxi, ma'am.'

She sat back. 'Okay. Fire away.'

'I've found two firms that sell retired taxis, ma'am. They each sell up to ten a year. So, it's a small market. People like them as they're safe, versatile and good in tight spaces.'

'Right. That makes sense.'

'But I've also found only one firm does the lion's share of insurance for these taxis. And they've agreed to give us a copy of their list of live clients. I'll collect it later today.'

'Wow. That's great, Barry. Well done.'

After he left, she felt a thrill at the prospect of finding a common address from the three lists. The taxi insurance list, the Nash Terrace addresses, and the thirty-seven leads on her wall. Fingers crossed.

***

Sandra thought Savills' offices oozed luxury. And John Howard, their Senior Partner contact, fitted right in. A tall, grey-haired man, with a tan. Just exuded trust.

They sat in armchairs around a low table beside the window. He smiled at them. 'I'm John. May I call you Sandra and Brian?'

Sandra nodded. 'Yes, of course.' *If she ever wanted to buy a high-end house, he was the man to see.*

'Thank you. From your call, Brian, you wanted info on houses that had a built-in trolley to service basement rooms. These are the brochures for two Nash Terrace houses I sold in the mid-1930s that had this feature.' He passed them over.

Sandra glanced through one of them. A very smart luxury home on five levels. 'This doesn't mention it.'

'We didn't see it as a good selling point.'

'Oh, I see. So, can we go back a bit, John? Can you tell us about Nash Terrace houses? And why they had this feature installed?'

'I can indeed, Sandra. Let me show you this.' He unfolded a map on the table. 'This is Central London. And here's Regent's Park. The term "Nash Terrace" describes the series of English terraced houses built around the park here.

'There are ten Terraces, with over two hundred large houses in total. Starting with Gloucester Gate, on the north-east of the Park. Then clockwise to Cumberland Terrace, Chester, Cambridge, York, Cornwall. Clarence, Sussex Place, Hanover and Kent in the south-west. All designed by John Nash and built in the 1820s.'

Sandra gasped. 'My gosh. I walked round that park at the weekend, and admired these houses. Wondered who lived in them.'

'Well, they're owned by wealthy people. Or large companies, who either house their staff or rent them out to other wealthy people.'

'And what about these built-in trolleys?

'Have you ever heard of the Spanish flu pandemic?' She shook her head. 'No.'

'It broke out in 1918, and swept around the world over the next two years. It blighted five hundred million people and caused over twenty million deaths. The worst pandemic for centuries. Dreadful.

'At its most extreme, people's lungs filled with fluid. They developed mahogany spots over their cheekbones, which then spread to a bluish colour all over the face. Then their hands and feet turned black, which spread to the rest of the body. Death followed shortly after.'

'My God. How do we not know about that?'

'The government at the time, still reeling from the First World War, controlled the press, and curbed comment on it. So, most people didn't know about it.'

'Out of sight. Out of mind.'

'Yeah. But the well-read and wealthy knew about it. They realised isolation could limit the spread.

'One Nash Terrace resident called in a local builder to convert his basement rooms for isolation. And this included a service trolley that could move food and other goods into and out of the room. With the wall sealed and locked again after each movement.

'The word spread, and other people copied the idea. I believe around thirty were installed. But once the pandemic passed, many owners removed them.

'These two houses I sold in the thirties still had them then. And there might well be others. Even elsewhere in London. But that house in Chester Terrace still had one eight months ago, when we concluded a new Lettings contract for an Australian banker. My colleague talked about it. Hope that helps.'

'It does indeed, John. Very helpful. And we appreciate your time. Thank you so much.'

'My pleasure. Is this a serious crime you've got?'

'Yeah. Pretty serious.'

'And I assume you want to keep your enquiries secret at this stage?'

'That's correct. Why do you ask?'

'Well, it's one of our key target areas in London. Has become a bit shabby over the war years. But we think owners will now put money into these houses and values will soar again. Could mean lots of good business for our Sales and Lettings.

'So, we're planning a marketing push. Call on each house. Promote our services. But it might help you too.'

'In what way?'

'Well, we could say something like, "Some people report a recent insect nest in their basement. While we're here, we could have a quick look and tell you if you're clear?" I think most people would take that.

'They get comfort on a problem and you get the info you're looking for. What do you think?'

Sandra pondered. *This guy could sell ice-creams to Eskimos.* 'What about the owners, though? I'd really like that info too. And how long would it take?'

'Maybe a couple of days? And we get the owners from the Land Registry.'

'Okay. Let's do it. Thank you.'

'You're welcome. Is there anything else you'd want us to check at the same time? Since you're from Special Branch, would you like to know any foreign aspects?'

'Well, now you mention it, we'd like to know any Russian links you trip over.'

He smiled. 'Okay, we'll do that for you as well.'

Sandra put the brochures into her bag and stood. 'Thank you, John. Good to meet you.'

'Likewise, Sandra. Get back to you later this week.'

'Thanks again.'

They shook hands, left the offices, and Brian asked, 'What do you think of that, ma'am?'

'Amazing man. No wonder they're so successful.'

***

On the way back to the office, Sandra leaned forward. 'Reg, could you take us round by Chester Terrace at Regent's Park, please?' She turned to Brian. 'Let's have a look at this trolley thing. I can't picture it.'

She and Brian walked up the steps and rang the doorbell. A maid answered. 'Good afternoon. We're from the police. May we speak to the man or woman of the house, please?' She gave her a card.

'Please come in. I'll get her for you, madam.'

They stood in the large entrance hall. A crystal chandelier above their heads. Luxury decor, furniture and carpets throughout. 'How the other half live, Brian?'

He smiled and nodded.

An elegant lady emerged from a door at the far side and approached them. Gorgeous silk dress. Greying hair styled. Hands out. And with a big smile. 'Hello. I'm Hattie Mulholland. Just call me Hattie. How can I help you?' *A broad Australian accent.*

Sandra and Brian introduced themselves and showed their warrant cards. 'We're involved in a case where we think a basement room had a trolley that served it with food, etc, during the Spanish flu nearly thirty years ago. But we've never seen one. Savills gave us this brochure of your house and said you had one of these here. Is it possible to have a look at it, please? See how it works?'

'Yeah. Sure. Come this way.' She led them through a door at the side of the hall, and down stairs into the basement. 'We only use this area for storage. But that's the trolley there.'

Sandra studied the structure. An assembly of steel tubes mounted on the wall at waist height and running down to a pair of wheels on the floor. She tried to pull it, but it wouldn't move.

Hattie stepped forward. 'Oh, you've got to lift this locking bar up here.' She did so, and the unit pulled out to reveal a two-foot square section with an open tray about two feet long, and the inside wall now butting against a seal half-way into the wall. 'I'm told the tray section used to have a cloth cover, but it's long gone.'

Sandra nodded. 'Can I see the other side?'

'Yes, of course.' Hattie opened the adjacent door.

Sandra looked in. The inside now looked like the outside did when she arrived. The room filled with boxes and spare tables and chairs.

'Okay. Thanks, Hattie. I've now got it.'

'You're welcome, Sandra. Any time.' She closed the unit from the outside, put the locking bar in place, and led the way back upstairs.

'I remember that Spanish flu outbreak. We married on New Year's Day, 1919, and lived in a small town north of Sydney. So, we were well away from it. But for the next six months, it ravaged our cities. We lost over ten thousand people to it.

'Nothing compared to you guys, of course. You lost twenty times that. No wonder people wanted to isolate.'

'Yeah. Must have been tragic.' They shook hands at the front door. 'We appreciate your time, Hattie. If there's ever anything I can do for you, just call me.'

'Will do, Sandra. Bye for now.'

They got into their car, and Sandra turned to Brian. 'At least we now know what we're looking for.'

***

Back at the office, Sandra flopped into her chair and buzzed her secretary. 'Any messages, Gayle?'

'Inspector Crichton wants to see you, ma'am.'

'Ask him to come in, please.'

'Yes, ma'am.'

She hung up and waved Brian to sit. 'Shit. Nothing from the bloody Russians.'

'Not easy to dump someone in daylight, ma'am.'

'Yeah. They won't use the Adelphi Hotel again.'

Barry knocked and came in. 'Got the list from the taxi insurance firm, ma'am. A hundred and twenty-one in the London area. Gives the reg number, owner's name and address, location, mileage, and various other info. Almost all of them owned by companies.'

'Let me see it?' He handed her several sheets of paper. She studied the entries. 'I assume "location" means where they keep the taxi?'

'Yes, think so, ma'am.'

She pulled her map of Central London from her bookcase, and passed it to Brian.

103

'Give me the names of the Nash Terraces, starting with Gloucester Gate and finishing at Kent Terrace, Brian. Let's see if there are any matches.'

He read them out, and she scanned the Location column, and marked a cross where it matched.

'That's seven matches. Wow! I like that.'

'Do you want to visit each one, ma'am?'

'No. If it was the right one, they wouldn't let us in without a warrant. Would just alert them. And we'd need other data to confirm the address to get a search warrant. It's too many to have a round-the-clock watch.'

'Barry. Take this list and see if there's a match with any of the thirty-seven addresses on the wall.'

'Will do, ma'am.' He left the room.

'Just feel we're getting closer, Brian.'

Ten minutes later, he returned. 'Sorry, ma'am. No matches between these seven locations and any address on the wall.'

She grimaced. 'Yeah. Maybe too easy? We'll see what Savills comes up with. Hope we get a match there. Okay, let's leave it at that. See you in the morning.'

They left the room. She sat and wondered when she'd get the call they had released Chuck. Maybe into the evening. Better get something to eat.

***

The call came just after ten. In the past hours, cycles of hope, worry, despair and reality had drained her. But now, she grabbed the phone. 'Hello?'

'Is that CS Sandra Maxwell?'

'It is.'

'This is Nurse Brent from the Royal Free Hospital.'

'Yes?'

'An ambulance has just dropped two people, a man and a woman. Both found unconscious, with envelopes addressed to you. That's why I'm calling.'

Man and woman? 'Do you have their names?'

'Charles Campbell and Lorna Mitchell.'

'What? I'll be right over.'

'Come to A&E, and ask for me.'

'Okay. See you soon.'

She dashed down to her car. *Lorna Mitchell? What the hell was she doing here? Should be in Spain?* Ten minutes later, she rushed into A&E. Within a few minutes, Nurse Brent appeared. 'CS Maxwell?'

'Yes. How are they?'

'Still unconscious.' They hurried into the clinical area. 'We think they've both had knock-out drops. But other than that, they're in good health. The woman has an injury to her right hand, and will need minor surgery.'

'What's the damage?'

'She's lost the tip of her fourth finger.'

'Oh, no.'

The nurse pulled a curtain aside. 'In here, we have Mr Campbell.' Sandra stood beside the bed and resisted her desire to lean over and kiss him. *Let's just keep my distance for the moment.* 'And here is the letter addressed to you.'

She tore the envelope open and read the typed note. 'This is from Glorious Russia (GR) again. As agreed, we have released Mr Campbell. We hope you have learned a lesson. Think twice before doing this again.'

She folded the note back into the envelope and put it in her bag. 'What will you do with him now?'

'We'll move him up to Ward Five within the next few minutes, and keep him overnight. But he should be ready to go home in the morning.'

'And what about the woman?'

'She's in the next cubicle.' The nurse closed the curtain on Chuck and opened the next one. 'And here's her letter for you.'

Sandra read the note. 'This is from Glorious Russia (GR) again. We know this woman betrayed her team mates in Glasgow. She deserves to pay for that. Now she'll have a constant reminder of her deceit. Her beauty reduced by just a tip.'

Bastards. One of the captured Russians had the same defect. So this sure would remind her.

Sandra put the letter in her bag. 'What about her?'

'She'll go to theatre for surgery within the hour. Again we'll keep her overnight, but she should also be ready to go home tomorrow.'

Sandra looked down at the tanned face. *Oh, Lorna, why did you come back? And how did GR find you?*

'Okay, we'll take care of that. Do you know where they were found?'

'Beside the staff entrance at the rear of Selfridges in Oxford Street. Around a quarter to ten.'

'Right. We'll follow that up. Thanks for your help.'

'You're welcome.'

Sandra left, got into her car, and sighed. *At least another step along the way. And precious Chuck back with her tomorrow.*

She picked up the phone, called Brian and updated him. 'I know in Glasgow the big stores had night shift staff in from ten to six. Get a team into Selfridges and see if it's the same there. And if anyone saw anything in the street tonight.'

Then she called her boss. Then Gary, Chuck's boss. They'd all meet to debrief Chuck next morning.

Chapter 9. Yellow Tuesday

Sandra told her team of last night's events. 'Anything from Selfridges, Brian?'

'Nothing useful, ma'am. We found the man who called the ambulance. He thought he saw two bundles of clothes near the entrance. Then realised it was two people out cold. No one else saw anything.

'It's a quiet street, used mostly by taxis as a shortcut between the big Park Lane hotels and the main stations at Euston and Kings Cross.'

'Mmm. Maybe another taxi link, huh?'

She went back to her office and called the hospital. They expected to release Chuck after the doctor's round. Around eleven. She then called her boss, Dave, and Gary at the CIA, to meet in her office at eleven-thirty.

Then she called Lynn Blackburn, the WP admin girl in Glasgow. 'Do you know where Lorna Mitchell is?'

'Yes. She's in Marbella. She moved to a hotel there a week ago.'

'How do you know that?'

'She left a message to call her last Monday. But I was out of town all day. So I called her at the Malaga hotel last Tuesday morning. My contact there, Miguel, told me she had checked out and gone to Marbella, just down the coast.

'She had left a second suitcase with them and he would send it on once he knew the new hotel. He said he would call me with the name. But he hasn't called, and I'm sorry, I haven't followed up. I'll call him now and get back to you.'

'No need for that. She's in London. In hospital. Found unconscious in the street last night.'

107

'Oh, my God. What happened? Is she okay?'

'Don't know the full story yet. But I'm guessing someone kidnapped her, injured her, and dumped her.'

'Injured her? How?'

'Cut off the tip of her fourth finger on her right hand. It's a long story. But I'll interview her later today and let you know how she is.'

'Oh, poor girl. Not much witness protection, huh?'

'Well, the girl herself might have broken the rules.'

'Need to think what we do with her now.'

'Okay. I'll call you again later.'

Sandra shook her head. Typical Lorna. Mind of her own. Impulsive. But why did she come back?

She then called Lenkov at the Russian Embassy. 'Thank you, ma'am, for getting our men to us on Friday. I hope this GR group delivered your men in return?'

'They didn't. Only one. Then demanded we stop looking for them. We agreed to that, and last night they delivered the other one. Plus the girl.'

'What girl?'

'The one this bloody group kidnapped and hurt. You must know who they are by now?'

'I'm sorry, ma'am. We know nothing about them. Nor about any girl.'

'I find that very hard to believe, Mr Lenkov. They seem to have access to details of what's going on inside your office. Only known by your senior staff. How do you explain that?'

'I can't, ma'am. I do accept it appears that way. But we've looked and can't find them.'

'Well, let me tell you. If we find them, and we will, their feet won't touch the ground on the way to prison, diplomatic immunity or not.' She hung up.

***

Sandra arrived at the nurse's station in Ward Five just on eleven o'clock.

'Can I help you, ma'am?'

'I'm here to collect Mr Campbell.'

'Oh, yes. He's ready to go. Are you his wife?'

Just keep it simple. 'Yes.'

'Doctor wants a word with you. I'll just get him.'

She went into a small side room, and emerged with a white-coated young man with a big smile.

'Mrs Campbell. I'm Doctor Jack. Your husband is clear for discharge. We think he's had a dose of sodium thiopental, a fairly new drug, or chloral hydrate, known in the US as a "Mickey Finn".

'Either way, there are no lasting side effects. Though his speech or thought might be a bit slow over the next twenty-four hours. He should then come back to normal. If you sense any other effects, please call us.'

'Thank you, doctor. Will do.' They shook hands, and the nurse guided her into the ward.

She saw Chuck sitting beside a bed, half-way up the ward, and smiled. He stood, and they hugged. 'Come on, darling, let's get you home.'

Chuck waved to the man in the next bed, and they left the ward hand-in-hand. In the elevator, she put her hand around his neck and kissed him. 'Oh, I've been so worried. Missed you like hell.'

'Yeah, me too, honey. Are we going home?'

'Got to stop by the office first. Gary and Dave want to see you. Make sure you're okay.'

'Right. Let's do that.'

She snuggled into him in the car, and fifteen minutes later, marched into her office.

Chuck said, 'Hey, guys. Good to see you.'

They all shook hands and sat round the table.

Sandra leaned forward. 'Doctor said he should take it easy for the next twenty-four hours.'

Gary nodded. 'We'll do that. Any idea where you've been for the last ten days, Chuck?'

'No idea, Gary. What happened to Greg? He was in the next room. Did he get freed on Friday?'

'He did. Now back at the airbase. He couldn't tell us anything either.'

'Thought it was a double swap?'

'Well, they demanded that Sandra stopped looking for them before they freed you.'

'Oh, I see. Didn't see or speak to anyone the whole time. Food arrived by trolley. Tried to keep fit and read books. Did we do the swap?'

'Yeah. On Friday.'

'Well, we knew it was going to happen.'

'Yeah. Let's put it all behind us and get back to business, huh? How do you feel? Back in the morning?'

'Fine. See you then.'

Dave said, 'Sandra and her team have put in a pile of work to find your captors. She tells me we're close.'

'Wow. That's great. Good to get them.'

Sandra sensed he was already getting tired. 'Think we'll get you up to the flat, have lunch and you can relax for the rest of the day.'

'Sounds good.'

Gary stood, shook hands, and left the room. And Dave went back to his office.

'Come on. Let's get you home. I'll let you know what we've done over lunch. Then you can relax. Read the *Sunday Times*. Or a book. Whatever you want.'

'Maybe go for a walk up Regent's Park? Get some fresh air. Enjoy the freedom.'

'Are you sure about that?'

'Well, let's see.'

***

At two o'clock, Sandra entered the hospital again, but this time went to the nurse's station in Ward Seven. She showed her warrant card. 'I'm here to collect Lorna Mitchell. I believe she's ready for discharge.'

'She is indeed, ma'am. Come this way.' They walked into the ward. 'Is she under arrest?'

'No, no. Just helping us with a case.'

'Oh, I see. You know why she's here?'

'Yes. I saw her last night. What was the outcome with her finger?'

'Our surgeon has reconstructed her finger. He cut back the bone a bit more to create a flap of skin, and sewed it over the wound. Best we could do without the tip. We've now put a dressing over it. She needs to come back in two weeks to get the stitches out.'

'Okay. Does she know that?'

'Yes. We've just told her.'

They stopped by the bed. Lorna looked up. 'Oh, ma'am, it's you?'

'Yes. Here to collect you and get you home.'

'Thank you.'

Sandra helped her gather her things, and they left the ward. On the way back to the car, Lorna asked, 'Are we going straight home?'

'No. We'll stop by my office first. I need to know what happened to you. And why you're back here?'

'Oh, of course.'

The journey passed in silence. They settled next to each other at Sandra's table. Her secretary brought in tea for two, and she began the interview. 'Could you tell me first why you left Spain and came to London?'

'Well, Spain wasn't for me, ma'am. The men were mostly sleazebags, and the women sad divorcees who only wanted to get a waiter into bed. Not my scene.'

'Well, you look better for it.'

'But you can't live on just sunshine, ma'am. And the one reasonable man I met ended up dead a week past Sunday. That was the last straw.'

'Wow. Who was he?'

'A guy from Glasgow I met on the first day. Alex Jardine. No romance or anything. Just good company.'

Jardine? From Glasgow? That rang a bell. 'What did he do to end up dead?'

'He started a business selling German happy pills through pharmacies along the Spanish coast. The police think a local Spaniard wanted to take over.'

German happy pills? More bells. 'Excuse me, Lorna. I just want to check something.' She picked up the phone. 'Gayle. Could you get me Tom Hamilton at Glasgow office, please?'

The line clicked. 'Hello, ma'am. How are you?'

'I'm fine, Tom. Could you check something for me, please? Remember about six months ago, the Aquila drugs job? Sam McFadden?'

'Yes, of course.'

'We found a new, unused passport in his desk in the name Andrew Jardine. Is that correct?'

'It is correct, ma'am.'

'Right. Remember the photo we took at Thomson's place on the cat camera? McFadden and Eddie Frame? Could you radio telegraph that down to me, and let Gayle know when you've done it, please?'

'Will do, ma'am.'

'Thanks.' She hung up and turned to Lorna. 'We'll talk about that in a few minutes. Now, did you have any other reason to come back here?'

'Well, I kind of like a rich man in my life, and Sir Anthony wanted to throw his hat in the ring. So I called him to see if he still felt the same. If he would like to meet me at the tearoom on Friday.

'He said he did, so I came back. But it didn't work out. His man, Snuff, told him I had too much baggage. So he walked away. Pity.'

'And where are you staying back here?'

'Oh, I was lucky. Got my old flat back from my lovely Swiss banker.'

'Mmm. You knew the rules, Lorna. You had to sever all ties from your old life. Now, you've paid the price.'

'How do you mean?'

'We found you unconscious outside Selfridges last night with an envelope addressed to me pinned to your dress. It had this note.' She passed it to her.

Lorna read it, put her hand up to her mouth, and then looked at her finger. 'Oh, my God. The same as Mariusz. Have you found this GR?'

'Not yet. But we think we're close.'

'Shit.' She grimaced. 'My fault.'

'Well, we know the Russian Embassy hired a private detective to find out what happened to their men, Peter and Mariusz. And he did a good job. But they didn't tell us everything he found.

'For example, I know they knew about you. But they never said that. So they might well have known about Sir Anthony as well, and followed him. You just fell into their lap when you saw him on Friday.'

'Shit. Sorry.'

'So, what happened on Friday? And how did they grab you? Tell me everything you remember.'

'Well, I didn't expect him to walk away. You know, he was the only man I ever met who admired me for my ability and not just my beauty.'

'How come?'

'During the war, when I worked for the War Office, I arranged a series of meetings for key suppliers where Churchill spoke and thanked them for their efforts.

'He attended one of these meetings. Told me he had admired me at that meeting. Had now divorced. Hence the interest.'

'You never told us that.'

'Well, I told you the meeting with him went well.'

'Mmm. So, what happened after he walked out?'

'I just went home and drowned my sorrows over the weekend. Then yesterday, gave myself a shake, and decided to have a walk in Hyde Park.

'I waited to cross Cromwell Road in the middle of a bunch of tourists, and just collapsed. I became woozy. A man shouted he was a doctor and examined me. He then shouted for a taxi to take us to the nearest hospital. Said to the driver, "You dash" or something like it, just as I blacked out. That's it till I woke in hospital.'

Another bloody taxi link. 'I can tell you someone injected you with knock-out drops. Sodium thiopental or chloral hydrate. They're fast-acting drugs with few side effects. So you'll fully recover by tomorrow. Did the hospital give you pain killers for your hand?'

'Yes, they did.'

'Okay, I'll take you home. And I'll call Lynn Blackburn and let her know where you are.'

'Oh, shit. I forgot to call her.'

'Well, she tried to get you on Tuesday. The Malaga hotel told her you had gone to another hotel in Marbella. You left a case for them to send on.'

'That's right. I didn't tell them about leaving Spain. The Malaga police had interviewed all the Brits at the hotel. And cleared us. But I didn't know whether they'd want to hold us there. Hence the Marbella story.'

'Well, Lynn may not keep you in the programme.' Gayle came in with the photo. Sandra folded it so that only Eddie Frame showed. 'Is this the man you knew as Alex Jardine?'

She gasped. 'That's him. How did you know?'

'We wanted him for a drug offence in Glasgow. Just ties up another loose end.'

'Oh, he was such a nice guy, too.'

'Yeah? Well, maybe too nice for that game. Come on, let's get you home.' Fifteen minutes later, they arrived at her flat in South Kensington. 'Really nice flat, Lorna. Do you live here alone?'

'Yes. Lived here for ten years. My Swiss banker lover has gone back home now, but I still pay him only a token rent. I'm very lucky.'

'What about your brother? That man Snuff told me about him. Part of the gang that attacked Preston on his yacht. You were lucky to avoid that one.'

'I suppose so. He's also lived here at times. But I won't see him now for at least ten years.'

'Have you contacted him?'

'No. I assumed you had a watch on any contacts. Don't even know what prison he's in. He understands.'

'Well, I better let you get on with the rest of your life. I'll call Lynn. But I think they'll remove you from the programme. Here's my card. Keep in touch.'

'Thanks. That man, Alex Jardine. I think he had a family in Glasgow. Will you let them know?'

'Yeah. We'll do that. Take care now.'

She went back to the office, called Lynn, and told her about Lorna.

'I've talked with my supervisor, ma'am. Unless you have a strong case to keep her in the programme, we will reverse her out. She can keep her new name and ID, but lose everything else.'

'That's fine. I agree with that.' She then called Tom in Glasgow. Told him about Alex Jardine, aka Eddie Frame, and that he should contact the Malaga police, then his family. Now time to get home to Chuck.

***

'Hi, love, I'm home.' She opened the door to the lounge. He rose and came towards her, arms wide, with a big smile. *Looked very relaxed. A real surprise.*

He hugged and kissed her. 'Hey, honey. Got your drink ready for you.' He gave her the glass. 'Cheers.'

She clinked glasses. 'Cheers. My goodness. You look good. Feel better already?'

'Yeah, feel terrific. Had a great day.'

They sat on the sofa. 'Wow. Tell me about it.'

'Here. Read this advert in the *Sunday Times*.'

She sat back and read it.

'Britain's Brand New Airline. BEA. Aiming to be Number One in Europe. Vacancies in all areas. Flight crew or ground operations. Call and discuss your new career with us.'

She looked up. 'So, you called them?'

'Sure did, honey. Said on paper, I'm gold dust. Meeting them Thursday evening. They've just pulled all airlines in Britain under the BEA banner. Already got their first six new Vickers Vikings of a total eighty.

'Have a base at Northolt for European flights and at Liverpool for domestic. But they plan to merge it all at a new airport at Heathrow, a mile south of Northolt.

'Blown over by my TWA experience. Over ten years, seven of them as a Captain. Just what they're looking for. They're seeing lots of ex-RAF flyers, but they lack the soft skills required for that role.

'They reckon if Thursday goes okay, I could be flying again as a Captain out of Northolt within three months. Short-haul into Europe. Lots of take-offs and landings. Real flying. Brilliant, huh?'

Her stomach knotted, but she couldn't show it. 'Wow. Sounds great. If that's what you want. What about Gary and the CIA?'

'Ah. The one good thing about the last ten days is it gave me time to think.

'I don't want to be part of this global chess game anymore. One side makes a move to gain an advantage. The other side responds with a move to offset it. All within unwritten rules.

'It's nuts. I'm a flyer, honey. Not an intelligence gatherer. It's just not me. And I need to get out. And this is my big chance to do it and live here with you.'

'Great. Let's follow through and see where it goes.' *She wouldn't burst his bubble. He needed to feel confident again.*

They went out for a quick meal, where he never stopped talking about BEA and the future. He never asked her about her day. Back to the flat where they made passionate love, which surprised her.

Out of the carnage of his kidnapping, his boyish enthusiasm had emerged again. And she liked that.

Chapter 10. Red Thursday

Sandra held her morning meeting in her 'war room'.
Hoped she'd find the missing link. From the leads on the
wall, the taxi insurance info, and the info from Savills
when it arrived.

'Just heard from Savills, lads. The info we asked for
is on its way. Brilliant.

'While we're waiting, Barry. Where are we with the
review of leads we got rid of?'

'Of the fifteen removed on Monday, we've now
confirmed twelve of them. But we've removed another
three since then. So we still have the same total of
twenty-two live leads.'

The team discussed their issues with these, and then
Gayle came in with the package from Savills.

Sandra tore open the envelope, and pulled out a
sheaf of papers. They listed each Nash Terrace house in
sequence from Gloucester Gate to Kent Terrace, the
owners, and those that had a trolley system in the
basement. There were only eight of these.

'Right, Barry. I'll read out these eight addresses.
You check them on the taxi insurance list. Any matches,
write them on the flip chart.'

There were two matches. One in Carlton Terrace and
one in Hanover Terrace.

Sandra grimaced. 'Shit. We need something else that
confirms one or other as our target. And we didn't have
any matches between the Terrace addresses and those on
the leads wall. So where do we get it?

'Let's look at the owners. For Carlton Terrace, it's
Mungall Holdings. For Hanover Terrace, it's Victoria
Point Investments. Any links there, Barry?'

'Yeah. I've seen that Victoria name somewhere in our leads.' He went through his files. 'Here it is. Lead eight. From the wife of one of our cops. Saw vodka bottles in her friend's flat. Jill Graham. In Islington. Interviewed last Wednesday at Barclays.

'Russian link? Her boyfriend, Dmitri Petrov. Interviewed at her flat last Wednesday evening. He was in Cambridge all day on the Friday. Waiting on feedback from the railway company on his tickets. Director of Victoria Point Investments. That's it. He's the link.'

Sandra banged the table. 'Right, Brian. Let's get search warrants for her flat and the Hanover Terrace house. My authority.

'Bring in the girl and the Russian, and anyone at the Hanover Terrace house. Check prints.' She paused. 'Hang on. An asterisk at the Hanover Terrace listing. What does that mean?' She scanned through to the last page. 'The asterisk is for the only possible Russian link they found. The housekeeper's name is Irina.

'Right. Let's go, go, go. Bring them in. Search the houses. Let's find the evidence, lads.'

***

She rang the doorbell and waited. A woman opened the door. 'Police! We have a warrant to search this house.' Two of her team held the woman and cuffed her hands behind her back. 'I'm CS Maxwell from Special Branch. You're under arrest on suspicion of kidnap, detention and assault. You have the right to remain silent, but anything you do say will be taken down and may be used in evidence. Do you understand?'

The woman looked dazed and said nothing. The team spread through the house as planned. Held and cuffed a man in the lower kitchen. Then let Barry and the other half of the team in the back door.

Sandra headed for the basement. Two rooms side by side, both with trolley service systems. Matched what she wanted to see.

She entered both rooms in turn. Empty. No sign of any recent captives. Chuck had described the furniture, so it had to be somewhere. She found it all in a third room, piled floor to ceiling. 'Right, Barry. Get the prints boys to check all these items. We're looking for prints from Chuck, Major Julich, or Lorna Mitchell.'

'Will do, ma'am. Just found a London taxi in the garage. Another box ticked. And we found this in the flat above the garage.' He handed her a framed certificate from the Royal British Legion Taxi-Drivers' Training School, Brixton, stating a Pass for the Knowledge of London in the name Igor Dubov.

'That's good, Barry. Yet another tick.'

She and Barry explored the rest of the house. Just as elegant as the Chester Terrace house she saw on Monday. Maybe even more so.

The ground floor had a huge lounge and dining room that linked to a garden room at the rear, with steps down to a landscaped garden with the garage at the far end.

The first floor had a smaller lounge / dining room to the front, with views across Regent's Park, and a master bedroom with en-suite at the rear.

The second floor had two bedrooms, front and rear, with a shared bathroom in the centre. The third floor had another bedroom to the front, a bathroom in the centre and a locked door marked 'Private' to the rear.

'Find the key for this, Barry. I'll phone Brian and see how he's getting on with the girl and the Russian.'

She went down to her car and called Brian's car. A few minutes later, he came on the line. 'We've got the girl, ma'am. Lifted her at her office in Barclays. She's in total shock. And I believe it's genuine.

'Petrov flew to Warsaw on Tuesday night, on his way back to Moscow. We've lost him, ma'am.'

'We're now at her flat. Checking for prints and any other evidence. Saw the two bottles of vodka in the sideboard our informant reported. One almost full. Gave us the idea that there might be an empty one in the trash. And we found it, ma'am. With two full right-hand prints. She's one of them, so we assume he's the other. We're happy with that, at least.'

'Brilliant, Brian. Bring her into the office. We've got two people here. The housekeeper and her husband. I'll do an initial interview with them here. Then bring them into the office as well. See you later. We'll cross-check what they say.'

She went back up to the third floor and found the 'Private' door open, with Barry checking the drawers in a desk and an adjacent filing cabinet.

'Looks like management papers for Victoria Point Investments, ma'am. Bedroom through there to the rear. Occupied by a male. Good quality clothes.'

'Right, Barry. Have the team box everything in this room, including the typewriter and blank paper. Keep each drawer separate. But first, get the prints boys to check every hard surface in these two rooms and the bathroom. Brian thinks he's got prints from Petrov at the girl's flat. We need to confirm them from here.

'In the meantime, let's go down and see what Mr Dubov has to say for himself.'

Barry passed on Sandra's instructions to the team lead for the upper floors, and they headed downstairs.

'Mr Dubov, I'm CS Maxwell and this is Inspector Crichton from the police Special Branch. We'd like to ask you a few questions to help with our enquiries.'

'No lawyer, no talk.'

She pursed her lips and studied him. Heavy-set and tough-looking. And this looked well-rehearsed. 'Okay, call your lawyer. Take his cuffs off.'

The officer standing behind him unlocked the cuffs and Dubov massaged his wrists. Then opened a black notebook on the table, checked a number, picked up the phone and asked for it. 'I'm Dubov from Victoria Point. I need a lawyer.' He paused, and checked the book. 'Yes. Reference number 037591.'

He paused again, then turned to Sandra. 'Where are you taking us?'

'Scotland Yard, Special Branch.'

He repeated her words. 'Okay.' He hung up. 'We talk there.'

'Fine. Who are your lawyers? We need to give them passes to get in and see you.'

He checked the notebook again. 'Josh Calman.'

Oh, shit. She'd heard that name before. The most expensive defence lawyers in the UK. Used by top business people and crooks. And lost few cases. 'Right, let's get going.'

'I need to call my daughter first. We look after all the VP properties, and we need her here to cover for us if we're away. And she needs to feed the dogs.'

'Okay. Call your daughter.'

He picked up the phone again, and spoke at length in Russian. He mentioned the names Petrov, Maxwell, and Scotland Yard. When he finished, he stood, put his hands out in front and the officer cuffed him again. They then headed for Scotland Yard with Igor Dubov and his wife, Irina, in separate cars.

***

Dmitri knocked the open door of his father's office, entered, and closed the door behind him. His father and sister smiled at him. 'Hey, Dmitri. You're back.'

'Yeah. Came in last night, dad.' He leaned over and kissed Nadya on both cheeks.

'Good result, Dmitri. The lads came back over the weekend. Still held at the Ministry. But the family's very happy. Well done. Everything go okay?'

'Think so. We lifted two Americans the previous Friday, and made a swap offer they couldn't refuse. This week covered our tracks. Cleared the basement, changed the typewriter, and wiped down all hard surfaces.

'But I've just had a call from Igor's daughter. That police woman, Maxwell, has just arrested Igor and Irina on suspicion of kidnap and detention. Surprised at that. Not sure how they would get the lead to our property. But we've already got Josh Calman on the job.'

'Good. He'll sort it out in no time. Anything else?'

'No. That's it.' *He wouldn't say anything about Jill Graham or the girl, Lorna Mitchell. They were personal.*

'Are they after you as well?'

'Don't know, dad. They had a purge on every known Russian last week. Interviewed me on Wednesday. So, I'm on their list. But didn't have any follow-up. I have to assume, though, if I'd been at the house, they'd have lifted me too. So, I'm maybe still a target.'

'Mmm. That's a pity. I need you to do an urgent job over there. What if we changed your appearance? Grow a beard? Get you a new ID? How about it?'

'What's the job? And how urgent is it?'

'You know we provide some funding for our atomic bomb project? Well, I had a meeting with Deputy PM Beria last week. He's in charge since the US dropped their bombs on Japan and gave us all a fright.

'He's pissed the Americans are so far ahead of us, and of course, he's also in charge of all our foreign intelligence activities. So, he's recruited spies in America who can feed us secret info on the technical aspects of their atomic bomb.

'One of his top spies has just moved to England, and he's asked us to fund the cash stream for him through our London embassy in the same way as the others. This can do us a lot of good in the right circles. Wants it in place within two weeks.'

'Yeah, I heard this could happen. But I think I'm too vulnerable if I go over there now, dad. They may have alerts out on me everywhere. I could organise most of it from here. Set up a new company for us in the BVI. Another new company for Mikhail. And Nadya could go over next week to slot the cash chain into place.'

'What do you think, Nadya?'

'Yeah. I could do that, dad. It would give Dmitri time to change his appearance and get a new ID. And time to appoint him as a new director of the company so he can operate properly. I'll do this trip, and Dmitri can follow up with maintenance visits in his new ID.'

'Right. Can you two get this set up now? I'll get back to Beria with the good news.'

***

Sandra flopped into her chair. Barry sat opposite. She buzzed her secretary. 'Any lawyers from the Josh Calman practice turned up yet, Gayle?'

'No, ma'am. I'll call you when they do.'

Brian knocked and came into her room. 'How did it go, ma'am? Find any prints?'

'Nothing when we left. Still hoping.'

'We're the same. Apart from the vodka bottle in the trash. Got lucky with that.'

'You make your own luck sometimes, Brian'

'Too true. Anyway, I've got some good news. From the train company. About Petrov's tickets on the sixth.'

'Let's hear it.'

'They've done their research on the clipped tickets. He must have taken an outbound train at 08.30 or 09,00. Couldn't have caught a later train. Yet he told us he had caught a train around ten.

'On the inbound, he must have taken the 18.00 or 18.30 from Cambridge. Again, couldn't be later. Yet he told us he caught one around 19.30. He lied both ways.

'Now I've checked if he could get to Marham by eleven. And he could. These trains to Cambridge go on to King's Lynn. He could've stayed on the train, bought another ticket from Cambridge to Downham Market, and had his taxi meet him at that station.

'It's about an hour to Cambridge. Another forty minutes or so to Downham Market, and another twenty minutes to Marham. So, with either train, he could get there by eleven. Cruise around and pick up an American. Major Julich. Then head back to Cambridge for his lunch meeting.

'Then, with his latest possible train from Cambridge, he could get into London before eight. Plenty of time to get over to the Brown Cow and pick up Chuck.

'Petrov is unique amongst all our leads, ma'am. He's the only one that *could* have done both kidnaps. And that makes him a *very* special person of interest.'

'Sure does, Brian. Good work. Now, neither Chuck nor Julich could identify the taxi driver. But we have Tony from the Brown Cow, and the gateman at the Adelphi Hotel car park. Let's have an ID parade with this lad, Igor. See if either picks him out.'

***

Her phone rang. Gayle. 'That's Josh Calman arrived, ma'am. With two others. They're talking with their clients, Igor and Irina Dubov, in separate rooms. He's also acting for the woman, Jill Graham. Wants to see you for ten minutes once he's finished.'

'That's fine, thanks.' She imagined him similar to Vince Pastrano, the most expensive defence lawyer in Scotland, whom she'd fought a few times. An ability to see cracks in her case and then find witnesses that could widen these cracks to chasms of reasonable doubt. And that's all he needed to win.

She had to have solid hard evidence, and she was a long way from that. Her present circumstantial evidence would not win it against him.

Half-an-hour later, he arrived. Medium height. Very well dressed. Hankie matching the tie flopping out of his top pocket. Longish hair going grey at the sides. Sharp eyes, and a big smile. 'CS Maxwell. Good to meet you. Heard a lot about you from my friend Vince Pastrano in Glasgow. Says you're a formidable foe. But firm and fair. Look forward to our future clashes.'

'Good to meet you too, Mr Calman.'

'Oh, call me Josh. I'm a very open person.'

'Fine. I'm Sandra.' They shook hands.

'Well now, thank you for seeing me, Sandra. Much appreciated. I act for both the Dubov couple and the girl, Jill Graham. Have you seen her?'

'Not yet.'

'She's in a bad way. Trembling. Can't think straight, or talk clearly. In total shock. And she knows nothing of Mr Petrov's detailed business activities, or the kidnap, detention and assault offences. I'd suggest, for her, there's simply no case, and you should let her go.'

Just like Pastrano's approach. Try to throw her off with the 'no case' argument.

126

'I can assure you, Josh, I'll interview her later today. If I find her wholly innocent, I won't hold her a second longer than I need to.'

'Thank you. I'm sure that's what will happen. As for the Dubov couple, they also claim no knowledge of the offences either. So they may be in the same position.

'I've advised them, unless you show hard evidence of their involvement, to give 'no comment' answers.'

'That's their legal right, of course. But I'd advise them to cooperate with us to prove their innocence. Otherwise, doubts will hang over them and their family as long as they remain in this country.'

'Is that a threat, Sandra?'

'Not at all. It's just a fact.'

'And what about Mr Dmitri Petrov? Would you have arrested him as well if he'd been at the house?'

Here he goes. Fishing for info about Petrov. To feed back to him. 'Yes, I would've done. But I understand he's now left the country. So, let's leave it at that and see where the evidence takes us.'

'Fair enough.' He splayed his hands. 'I'll leave you to get on with it. Pleasure meeting you, Sandra.'

'You too.' She buzzed Gayle to show him out.

An initial skirmish. No doubt he'd go over well in court. So we need to find hard evidence on this lot.

***

They walked downstairs towards the interview rooms. 'What's she like, Brian?'

'In a bit of a state, ma'am. Very shaky and nervous. We need to calm her down to get her to talk.'

'Okay, we'll do that.'

'How did it go with Calman?'

'Oh, typical. He starts with no case to answer. And goes on from there. We need hard evidence, Brian.'

As they went into the interview room, Sandra thought the girl almost jumped from her chair. *Very nervous. Do indeed need to calm her first.*

'Good afternoon, Miss Graham. I'm CS Sandra Maxwell. You've already met my colleague, CI Brian Walker. We would like you to help with our enquiries into your friend Dmitri Petrov. Is that okay with you? May I call you Jill?'

The girl nodded, still trembling. The female lawyer beside her said, 'We've agreed with Mr Calman that Jill should cooperate fully with you at this stage'

'Fine. Before we talk about Mr Petrov, let's talk about you.' *Try to get her to relax.* 'Where did you grow up? Are you a London girl?'

'Erm, no. I grew up in Torquay, Devon. My parents run a small hotel.'

'Oh? I've never been there, but I believe it's a very nice place for a holiday. Tell me about your early life and how you came to London.'

'Well, when I left school, I worked in the hotel. On the admin side. My elder sister did front of house duties. But I preferred the back room tasks.

'We used to go dancing twice a week. One night I met a boy from London on holiday. He made me laugh. We had a whirlwind romance, married within months, and moved to London. What a mistake that was.'

'Oh? Why was that?'

'We lived with his parents. But his mother hated me. We then got our own little flat. He was a salesman, and had big ideas for success. But none of them paid off.

'Then it all went downhill. We had fierce rows over nothing. Like I didn't iron his shirt as good as his mum, for example. And one night, he thumped me. I cracked an arm on a chair. That was the end.'

'My goodness. Sounds awful.'

'It was. I had a good job as a secretary with Barclays and earned more than him most weeks. So I divorced him for cruelty, and got my own flat.'

'Good for you.'

'Thanks. But the whole messy business shattered my confidence. I just closed in on myself. Then one night, working late, I met Dee. Mr Petrov.

'He sometimes used one of our offices when he was in town, and needed to find some detailed info about his account. He asked me to help.

'I did so. He was really nice, and invited me to dinner as a thank you. And it just developed from there. We get on really well together. Have similar interests in music, theatre, opera, and just going places. He really gave me back my confidence.

'I got a promotion into another department. So there was now no conflict with his position as a client. And it's been good.

'Oh, I know he has a wife and family in Moscow. But I'm easy with that. It's great having him close. I love his attention. But also like my freedom.

'And we never talk business. When he's here, he stays overnight most nights. He has an office elsewhere, but I don't know where. We have a good rapport that I enjoy very much.

'But this has been a total shock to me. And to be honest, I just don't believe he would kidnap, detain or assault anyone. For me, it's just not possible. I mean, how did you even think he could do that?'

She seemed a lot more relaxed now. 'Well, I won't go into details on that. But I can tell you that a serious offence occurred, which we thought was caused by someone with a Russian link. So we did a trawl for such people in London, and caught him in the net along with almost forty others.

'Since then, we've found further evidence that point to him being involved. We would like to discuss some of that with you.'

'Okay. So, how can I help?'

'You told Brian and his team that on Friday the sixth, Mr Petrov was still at your flat when you left just after eight in the morning. And he returned just before ten at night. Is that correct?'

'It is.'

'What was his manner when he returned?'

'High spirits. He'd spent the day in Cambridge and secured an investment in something that might generate huge profits for his company.'

'Do you know what that is?'

'No. He didn't go into details.'

'And can you remember how he was last Friday and last Monday?'

She thought for a moment. 'Same as always.'

'Was he late home on Monday?'

'Yes. He had a business dinner that evening.'

'Okay. And then he flew out Tuesday.'

'Well, that was his plan.'

'No, no. He *did* fly to Warsaw. We confirmed it. Do you know when he's due back?'

'I'm sorry, I don't. Recently, it's been every three or six weeks. But he didn't say this time.'

'You have a mutual interest in music and theatre. Did you go out to concerts or plays regularly?'

'Not much during the week. But often at weekends.'

'Did you take a taxi to these venues?'

'No. I'm within ten minutes of King's Cross. It's easy to get to anywhere in London from there. We just usually took the tube or walked.'

'Did you ever share a taxi with him?'

She shook her head. 'Maybe once, on a wet night? Why, is that important?'

'Well, it might have been.' *She wouldn't get much more from this girl. Calman was right, dammit.*

'So, what will you do now he's gone?'

She shrugged. 'Back to normal, I suppose. Meet friends again at weekends.'

'Good. Have you any plans to leave London in the next few weeks?'

'None at all.'

'If you do have to leave for any reason, please call me and let me know where and when. Here's my card. Is there anything you want to ask me?'

'When can I get back into my flat?'

Sandra turned to Brian. 'We should finish our checks by six at the latest. Then you can go back.'

'Okay, thanks. It's a huge shock for me.'

Sandra nodded. 'I'm sure it is. Not easy when you get caught up in other people's problems.'

The female lawyer asked, 'Does that mean you will not be charging my client with any offence?'

'At this stage, yes. She's free to go.'

'Thank you.' They gathered their things and left.

Sandra grimaced. 'Thought we had another potential witness for this taxi driver ID parade, but sadly not. How are we doing with it?'

'We should be almost ready. Do you want to come down and observe?'

'Yes, of course.'

They stood behind a one-way mirror, looking into the room. Five men stood in a line. Then an officer brought in Igor Dubov, and he selected a position.

Tony, the assistant manager at the Brown Cow, came in first, walked up and down the line, and shook his head. The gateman from the Adelphi had the same result. Neither recognised Dubov. *Dammit.*

'Shit. Not going to be easy, Brian. Find out the latest from the house, and come up to my office.'

He arrived ten minutes later. 'Any hard evidence?'

'Not a thing, ma'am. No prints from Chuck, Greg, or the girl, Lorna. Well wiped clean. No evidence they were ever there.

'Best potential link we've got is Dubov's black sweater, which he may have worn the night they lifted Chuck. We'll check it for traces off Chuck's sports jacket, but forensics say it's recently been laundered, so don't hold too much hope.'

'We haven't got it wrong, Brian, so how can we nail them down? Can we even link Petrov to the house?'

'We can, ma'am. He's signed documents there as a Director of Victoria Point Investments, and we picked up his prints off a file that match the vodka bottle.'

'Well, at least, that's something. But they cut the girl's fingertip off. Surely that would leave evidence?'

'I've asked the team to look for that in the kitchen or bathrooms. But so far, nothing. I assume they flushed the tip down the toilet and deep cleaned any blood away.'

'Have we checked the typewriter yet?'

'Yes, ma'am. Not a match for the GR notes. Nor the notepaper.'

'Mmm. Well, unless we find hard evidence, we don't have a case. Circumstantial won't cut it. Not with Calman around.'

'I know. His lawyers with Igor and Irina Dubov have already told us they won't answer questions unless we present evidence. Maybe not even then.'

'Well, that's their right. So let's keep looking. Have we got all these files over here yet?'

'Yes, ma'am. In the room next to the war room. Will they help with this case, though? Kidnap and assault?''

'Well, forensic accountants might give us something we can use for leverage. Fingers crossed.'

***

Lorna relaxed in her armchair to have lunch and listen to Workers' Playtime on the radio. Then the phone rang. She picked up. 'Hello?'

'Is that Cathie, Alex's sister?' *Glasgow accent.*

'Who wants to know?'

'Rab Dunn. Got a letter for you.'

'From Alex?'

'Aye. Smuggled it out the prison for you.'

'Where are you?'

'In the phone box opposite your flat. Don't see your name on the board. Don't know what flat you're in.'

Don't want him up here. 'Give me five minutes and I'll come and meet you.' *Need to dress down for this.* 'I'll wear a grey raincoat and headscarf.'

'Okay. See you then.' He hung up.

She stowed her lunch in the kitchen, got ready, left the flat, and walked towards him, standing next to the phone box. A short stocky man in an old gabardine coat and flat cap. And with a battered case at his feet.

'Hello, Rab.'

He shook her hand. 'Alex said you were a smasher.'

She smiled. 'Let's go to a café. We can talk there.'

'That's good. I'm just off the train.'

They walked to a café just past the tube station. Owned by Lily, a middle-aged Glasgow woman, who Lorna saw as a friend. They settled at a table at the back of the shop. Lorna ordered an all-day breakfast for Rab, and tea and a sandwich for herself.

'You've got a letter for me?'

'I do.' He went into an inside jacket pocket and pulled out an envelope that looked folded many times. 'He says to tell you he knows why you don't contact him. And it's okay.'

She opened the envelope and read the enclosed note in his familiar handwriting. Her heart thumped as she realised how much she missed him.

'Hello, sis. Hope this gets to you okay. I'm doing fine. Getting by. It's only time and it'll end one day. Rab's a good guy. My cellmate for the last six months. There's a lot more to him than you think. Used to do what we did. And good at it too. Caught the same way we did. By a random camera. So use him the same as me if you need to. Take as much of my money as you need to kit him out and get him into a B&B. He's a plumber to trade. So see if you can get him a job down there. He wants to be independent again. But take him under your wing and get him back on his feet. Use my money to keep him going if he needs it. I owe him a lot. Still got lots of happy thoughts about what we did. Good fun, eh? Look forward to seeing you again one day. Your loving brother, Alex.'

She read it again. Just like him sitting beside her. 'Do you know what's in this, Rab?'

'No. But he said you'd help me.'

'I will. He also says he owes you a lot.'

'Well, we looked after each other. A lot of violent nutcases in Peterhead.'

'Will he be okay now you're away?'

'Oh, yeah. He's got some good mates there.'

'Okay. He's asked me to do three things for you. Kit you out. Find a place to stay. And help you get a job. Are you happy for me to do that?'

'Would be great if you could.'

'Right. Where would you like to stay? A B&B? Or a hotel? Or your own flat?'

'I rented my own wee room and kitchen in Glasgow. Was quite happy with that.'

She glanced across. Lily leaned on the counter, reading a paper. 'Excuse me a sec.' She went over. 'Can I ask you something, Lily?'

'Of course.'

'Want to find a furnished one-bedroom flat for my friend from Glasgow. He's a plumber. What nearest area would be best for him? It's too posh around here.'

She thought for a moment. 'Even Earl's Court might be too posh. I'd go for Hammersmith. More working class. And only five stations away.

'I've also got their local weekly paper here. And here's the early edition of the *Standard* as well.'

Lorna took the papers back to her table. 'Right. Let's see what we can find for you.' She scanned the *Standard* for a furnished one-bedroom in Hammersmith. About a dozen listed with a basic description and letting agent's address. The same in the local paper.

They would have to go to a letting agent to get details, so she'd need to tidy Rab up first. Both papers also listed vacancies for plumbers. So getting a job might not be too difficult, if everything else was right. 'Are you a fully qualified plumber, Rab?'

'Yeah. I did a five-year apprenticeship. Got my lines here with me. I was bloody good too.'

'Okay. So, how do we cover for your prison term? How many years did you do anyway?'

'Three years. Stupid. Helped a mate to nick some valuable war material. But there was a secret camera. Stupid. But I just found out the company I worked for has gone bust. So, I hope I could get away with saying I'm looking for a job down here because of it. Which is kind of true. Just don't want to mention the prison bit.'

'Yeah. That might work. Is there anything else you want to do in your off-work time?'

'Well, I've kept myself fit in prison. But I used to be a pretty good gymnast. I'd like to get back to that again.'

'Okay. And what about social life? Women?'

'I think I'm too independent to get married. But I do like women's company more than men's.'

'Right. Let's take some notes on what we want to do.' She pulled out a notebook. 'First, spruce you up. Haircut. Decent shave. Then Marks and Spencer. Six sets of underwear and socks. Do you want a suit?'

'I'm no' a suit type of guy, Cathie. Just a couple of casual outfits and a couple of work outfits.'

'Okay. Plus toiletries in Boots. Maybe twenty quid total for that lot. Deposit and a month's rent in advance for a flat. Maybe another twenty. Spending money for food and drink till you're paid. Say another ten.

'And we'll get you a new case and tool bag. Right, let's note all these letting agents and plumber jobs.' She copied them from the newspapers in a preferred order. 'Okay, let's go.' She gave the papers back to Lily.

They first went to her bank and lifted sixty pounds cash in fives and ones, which she gave him. Then caught the tube along to Hammersmith.

Within two hours, he had spruced up, bought all his outfits and toiletries, ditched his old case and clothes, and was ready for letting agents and job interviews. Lorna had to admit he scrubbed up well. A bright, intelligent, well-mannered little man.

In their first letting agency, they struck gold. The advertised flat was close to the station. One of four in a large villa converted by a local builder.

When the agent heard Rab was a qualified plumber, she called the owner, who talked with Rab, and offered him the same deal as the previous tenant. A joiner who had worked for his company, done routine repair tasks at the villa, and reassured the other three female tenants with his presence. The photos looked great, and Rab signed the deal there and then.

They agreed to meet again at Lily's café at one o'clock on Saturday to check how he was doing.

***

Later in the afternoon, Brian came into Sandra's office. 'That's us got info back from forensics, ma'am. No links between the Dubovs or the house with Chuck, Greg Julich, or Lorna.'

'So, nothing from the black sweater, then?'

'Not a thing. Do you still want to question them?'

Sandra grimaced. 'Don't think so, Brian. I don't want to reveal the circumstantial evidence we do have. But they're bloody clever. Without hard evidence, we don't have a case. Let's just release them.'

Then her phone rang. *Her secretary, Gayle.* 'That's Clive Semple from Coopers & Lybrand here to see you, ma'am.' *The lead on the forensics accounting team.*

'Show him in, please.' She turned to Brian. 'Let's hear what he has to say first.'

Clive entered and sat. *Mid-forties. Hair going grey. Glasses. Very much the accountant.* 'Hi, Sandra. We've gone through the files from Victoria Point Investments. I'd like to give you some initial feedback.'

'Fine. Go ahead.'

'First, they only keep summary accounts here. The minimum they need to have on hand. So we can't see details of their activities.

'There are two sides to this business that we'd call "Open" and "Closed". Let's start with the Open side. This is the main business of Victoria Point.

'Started in 1935. They've invested large sums in property and technology. On property, they have a block of twelve luxury apartments near Hyde Park, and two adjacent luxury Nash Terrace houses near Regent's Park. They have a very high return from these rentals.

'On technology, they have eight projects at various stages, which seem to follow the same pattern. Concept; Detail; Launch; and Operations.

'On each project, they work with a top university on an advanced technical concept. If successful, they launch with a registered UK company, owned by the university, in which they take a twenty-four percent stake.

'They fund each stage of the process against targets. Some projects have failed at the early stages.

'Their most successful project to date has been the first, which developed a cavity magnetron that allowed small units to transmit and receive radio waves. It has generated a huge return on their investment.

'We've no details on how this was used. But clearly it was something that expanded hugely during the war.

'Projects two and three followed a similar, but less successful pattern. They ditched project four in 1939.

'The other four projects have all begun since late last year, and are still at an early stage. But this Open side of the business is highly self-funding at this time.'

'Is there any technology they focus on?'

'I'd say communications and miniaturisation.'

'Mmm. And what about the Closed side?'

'Well, this is very different. They have three businesses here, called VP1, VP2 and VP3, set up in the late 1930s, and all registered again in the British Virgin Islands. So we can't see who owns them.

'Each of these provides monthly transfers of twenty pounds to other BVI companies, ML1, ML2 and ML3, respectively. We've no idea what they do.

'They all seem to operate the same way, except that late last year, VP3 also transferred fifteen hundred pounds to ML3. But we've no details.

'And the only unusual thing we found anywhere was this folded receipt stuck in the bottom of a VP3 file.'

Sandra looked at the paper. From Soho Books. Rare Books Specialists. "A Fair Price Either Way". Receipt for "Nicholas Nickleby First Edition 1839 by Chapman & Hall. £9.0.0." Dated, 7th December, 1945.

She turned it over. A handwritten "Zapp", encircled. 'Hell of an expensive book, don't you think?'

Clive shrugged. 'People buy them as investments. It's a First Edition. Very rare. And as time goes on, it gets even rarer, so the value increases.'

'And what does Zapp mean? Do we know?'

'We don't. Never heard of it. I think this receipt fell into the file by accident. It wasn't a filed copy.'

'Okay, thanks Clive. Very useful.'

He stood. 'Good. I'll send our report in a couple of days. But I don't expect to have anything else to add. Sorry there's not more detail, but that's the way these BVI companies work.' He left.

Sandra turned to Brian. 'Nothing here that helps our case. Just release the Dubovs.'

He picked up the phone and gave the instructions.

Sandra sat and looked at the receipt. Who had bought that rare book? And why? Was it Petrov? He ran a very successful investment business and probably earned a bundle. Would he really see a rare book at nine pounds as a good personal investment? Didn't seem to fit. Or was it Dubov? Didn't fit even more.

Brian hung up the phone. 'That's them on the way, ma'am. I'm sure you'll hear from Josh Calman soon.'

'Yeah, of course. What about Jill Graham? Is she back in her flat yet?'

'Should be, ma'am. I called her before I came in here to tell her we had cleared her flat.'

Sandra asked her secretary to connect her, and a minute later, she came on the line.

'Jill? This is Sandra Maxwell here again. Thanks for your cooperation today. I just have another question for you. Do you have a minute?'

'Yes. What is it?'

'In December last year, did you ever see Mr Petrov with a rare copy of the book, Nicholas Nickleby?'

'I do remember that. I asked him if it was a good read. But it wasn't for reading, it was for an experiment, he said. I asked him what kind of experiment, but he just brushed me off. Just a bit of business, he said.'

'Thanks, Jill. I'd appreciate if you didn't mention this conversation to Mr Petrov.'

'Oh, that won't happen. I've already called him and broke off our relationship.'

'Probably for the best. What will you do now?'

'Oh, my friend at work has organised a blind date with her and her husband on Saturday. To help me get over the trauma. So we'll see what happens.'

Sandra chuckled. 'Good for you. Keep in touch.' She hung up and turned to Brian. 'It's a nice day. How about a walk up to Soho? I'd like to see this bookshop.'

'Yeah, good idea. Let's do it.'

Fifteen minutes later, they strolled along Wardour Street past the Soho Books shop. 'You wait here, Brian. I'll go in and have a browse.'

She entered, and passed the serving area to the left. The shop then opened up beyond that into a larger area, with shelves floor to ceiling, packed with old books. It had a very distinctive musty smell. She had no doubt it was a genuine seller of rare books.

A man with his shirt sleeves rolled up approached her. 'Can I help you, ma'am? Are you looking for anything in particular?' *White hair. Fifties? Healthy looking. Pleasant smile.*

'No, just browsing. A friend told me about investing in rare books. I'd never heard of it. Saw the sign outside and just popped in to find out more about it.'

'Ah, well. You've come to the right place. Most people find investments in rare books work well. It's a tangible asset, unlike stocks and shares, that you can take pride in owning. Easily stored at home.

'And the market doesn't suffer wild swings. As a rule of thumb, your investment in a rare book doubles every seven years. Some do even better.

'Collect an author or subject that excites you. That adds to the pleasure. When you're ready, come and see me. Been here over twenty years. Here's my card.'

She looked at it. *Peter Kent*. 'Thanks, I will.'

***

'Hey, honey, I'm home.'

She looked up from the sofa as he came in from the hall, and smiled. 'How did it go?'

'Wow. These guys at BEA are going full blast. All UK airlines have now come under the BEA banner. Plan to be number one airline in Europe by 1950.

'They've already started deliveries of eighty-three new Vickers Viking aircraft to link London with the major cities of the UK and across Europe.

'Really impressed with their recruitment process at Northolt. Divided into five groups. Flight Crew; Cabin Crew; Customer Services; Technical Services and Business Services. And lots of people there.

'Interview went well. Two Senior Captains. Checked my flying logs. Blown away by my TWA experience. Just what they want. Focused on problem solving and achievements in both TWA and USAAF.

'They offered me a job as Captain, subject to clean references and medical check. The money's slightly up on what I get. So I accepted.'

'Wow. That's great. When do you start?'

'The next training course starts in two weeks. On October 7. They'd like me to join that if I could. They called Martin, my boss at TWA. Gave me a glowing reference. Said he would have me back in a heartbeat.

'They had a doctor there who gave me a medical check. First class. And arranged a car to their local hospital for an X-ray. So, all good, huh?'

141

'Brilliant.' *He was back to his old self again. But she had to ask.* 'What will Gary say?'

'I'm hoping, given recent events, he'll let me go two weeks early. Could be flying again by New Year.'

'Let's hope he does.' She kissed him, and smiled.

Chapter 11. Aftermath

Next morning, Sandra met with her five managers plus Barry in her war room, and brought them up-to-date on the events of Thursday. 'We know we have the right gang, but just can't prove it. Don't feel bad. We know that happens. Our info cross-checks from the wall, the taxi insurance company, and Savills.

'We know, from the railway company ticket checks, that Petrov lied to us about his movements on the sixth. He *could* have kidnapped both Chuck and Greg Julich. But without hard evidence, we've no case.

'And I don't want to disclose to Calman what we do have. Let's keep them guessing. We've got alerts active at all ports for Dmitri Petrov. So if he comes back here, we'll lift him and give him a fright. But we have to face it. We won't get him into jail.'

Then Gayle, her secretary, came in with a note. "Commander Burnett wants to see you and Brian now."

'Sorry, lads. The boss wants to see Brian and me. Let's meet at four to review clear-up times. Thanks.'

They left and went to Burnett's office. Another man sat with him at the conference table. Late forties maybe? Dark hair. *Looked ordinary somehow*.

'Come in, you two. This is Eliot Forbes, a Director with MI5. Eliot, this is Sandra Maxwell, our new lead in London, and Brian Walker.' They all shook hands. 'Sometimes, guys, our investigations overlap with MI5, and when that happens, we get together so that neither buggers up the other's work.

'Yesterday, you two visited a bookshop in Soho that one of Eliot's teams had under obs. We want to find out why. Eliot, could you give us the background, please?'

143

'Yeah, thanks, Dave. Over the last twenty years, the Admiralty has developed devices that use echoes of sound waves sent out under water, to detect the position of submarines in order to attack them. They're called ASDIC systems, and very secret.

'During the war, their use became critical, and we worked with the US on further advanced technologies. We believe we're leading the world on this equipment, and do all our research and development at Portland on the south coast.

'Early this year, we picked up from spies that Russia had carried out an experiment on similar equipment that failed. Now, of course, all major military powers will develop such equipment as best they can. But that failure exactly replicated a similar failure by our Portland guys a few months earlier.

'Alarm bells rang we had a leak. So we started to keep an eye on the relevant staff. We have three under surveillance, called A, B, and C, with teams on each to find any suspicious patterns of behaviour or contacts.

'One of those, Mr B, brings his girlfriend up to London on a Saturday, once a month. They do some shopping, have dinner, do a West End theatre show, stay overnight at the Charing Cross Hotel, and travel back on the Sunday. Nothing suspicious, huh?

'Until one of our sharp-eyed team thought the man sitting next to Mr B in the theatre had also sat next to him in a different theatre a month earlier. He's now there on every occasion. But, other than some polite chat before the show, which looks normal, we've seen no communication between them. Of course, with the lights down, they could easily pass info.

So, we now have a team on him too. We think he's a Canadian national, who buys the three tickets for cash, and leaves two of them for Mr B to collect.

'He lives in a rented flat in Soho, and runs a small estate agent's business there. We've also noted that, on the Monday following his visit to the theatre, he browses a bookshop in Soho. But never buys anything. It's the only time he goes there. So, we've put that bookshop under surveillance as well.

'And yesterday we saw you two approach the shop, pause, and you went in, ma'am. One of our team knew Brian, and we realised who you were. We'd very much like to know why you visited.'

Sandra thought for a moment. *Let's be concise here.* 'Okay. We've had a recent case where we think a Russian businessman kidnapped two US citizens. Then bartered them with US authorities for two Russians they had extradited from here for the murder of a US citizen in Rome.' Eliot took notes as she spoke.

'We gathered enough evidence for a warrant, and raided his two known addresses here. But we missed him. He'd already flown back to Moscow.

'His name is Dmitri Petrov, and he's the Director of a company called Victoria Point Investments, set up in the British Virgin Islands. We have an alert at all ports for him, should he ever return.

'So far, we've found no hard evidence that links this Russian to the two kidnap victims. And his staff here admits nothing.

'During the raids, we pulled in the company files. But because of the BVI link, we have only limited info. So we called in forensic accountants to see if we could get any other evidence that might help us.

'They told us the company has two parts. A very successful open part that invests in technical initiatives in the UK. And a closed part comprising three other BVI companies, VP1, 2 and 3, each of which provides monthly payments to three other BVI companies, known as ML1, 2 and 3.

'We have no further info on any of these closed companies. But in the VP3 file, they found a folded receipt from the Soho bookshop for a rare book.

'It seemed to me unlikely this very rich Russian would invest in such a book. So I called his girlfriend here, who told me he had made an off-the-cuff remark the book was for a business experiment.

'Intrigued by all this, I decided to check if this bookshop was genuine, and so visited yesterday. I pretended I had heard that investing in rare books was a good thing and wanted to know more about it.

'I met the Proprietor, I think, who told me about investing, and to check back with him when I wanted to start. To me, the bookshop was indeed genuine.'

Eliot looked up. 'Do you still have the receipt?'

'Yes. I'll get it for you.' She popped along to her office and came back in a minute. 'Here you are. This is the man I met. And here's the receipt.'

He looked at the card. 'Yes. He and his wife have owned that business for twenty years.' He looked at the receipt. 'Seventh of December. Wow.'

'There's something written on the back.'

He turned it over. 'Zapp?' He thought for a moment. 'Can I use your phone, Dave?'

'Of course. Help yourself.'

Eliot asked for a number and waited. 'Patrick? It's Eliot here. Yeah, I'm fine, thanks. Remember, we had a technical update meeting in January? That's right. You told us about a guy called Zapp. Yeah, in Dresden.' He took notes. 'What did he do again? Oh, right. And how much did it cost? Okay, thanks. No, I'll tell you all about it later. Cheers.' He hung up.

'You'll gather he's one of our technical boffins. He says last year, this man Kurt Zapp in Dresden developed equipment to produce microdots. That's where they reduce a page of printed paper to the size of a full stop.

'He taught Russian spies how to use it so they could send a secret document as a full stop in a book. The Zapp outfit cost around five thousand dollars.'

Sandra cut in. 'That's interesting. Because the VP3 company paid the ML3 company a one-off fifteen hundred pounds last year. About six thousand dollars.'

'Wow, Sandra. That gives us a working hypothesis that the closed VP companies fund Russian spies via these ML companies. And ML3 could be this bookshop. And that money paid for a Zapp outfit to send secret documents as a full stop in a rare book. Sound plausible?

'ML1 could be our Mr B in Portland, and ML2 our Canadian national. I think that fits. The cash chain that holds this lot together. A great find. But we're a long way off proving it. And it's all organised by someone somewhere who links to your man Petrov. Do you know if he's met anyone while he's been here?'

'The only person we know he met is Professor James Cawthorne at Cambridge University.'

'Good. We'll check him out.'

Sandra smiled. 'It would be great to capture every link in the chain and close it all down at one blow.'

'Well, it doesn't always work that way, Sandra. Sometimes we let the chain run, but feed it false info.'

Dave scoffed. 'We'll leave that to you, Eliot. But it sounds as though our brush with the Russians may have uncovered something really useful for you, huh?'

'Yeah, it does. And I'm really chuffed about that. So, let's keep swapping notes on this.' He gathered up his papers, shook hands with them all, and left.

Dave sat back. 'Well done, you two. Good job. Hope this Petrov chap comes back here, Sandra.'

'If he does, we'll catch him. But with a different ID, that might be difficult.'

***

At four o'clock, Sandra reviewed clear-up times with her team plus Barry. She wanted him involved. He'd done a great job on the initial analysis, and on the wall.

He'd also replace her weakest head once she'd found another job for him. And in the longer term, could well take over from her. A talent to nurture.

She aimed to halve her present clear-up times, and hoped her new focus on them would help. But she also wanted to hear their ideas.

'Right, lads. We need to figure out how we can work in parallel with other regions and the Foreign Office to reduce clear-up times. What do you think? Any ideas?'

After a hesitant start, they discussed their ideas and settled on a single point of contact within each region and the FO to manage activities and results.

They proposed Barry as the POC for their London region, and Sandra agreed to have the boss force other regions to do the same. Barry agreed to use his analysis sheets as a starting point and propose how he would work with each division.

She wanted to get away early and concluded the meeting. 'Let's get our plans into place on Monday, lads. Have a good weekend.'

At home, she prepared drinks and waited for Chuck to arrive.

'How did it go with Gary?'

'A bit surprised. But he accepted my isolation had changed my thinking and wished me all the best. And he's agreed I can leave in a couple of weeks to join the training programme at BEA. So, I'm pretty happy about it all.' He raised his glass. 'Here's to my new career.'

She leaned over and kissed him. 'Cheers.' *Just keep supporting him through all this.*

***

On Saturday, at one o'clock, Lorna entered Lily's café. Rab sat at the same table as before. He looked dapper in his sports jacket and flannels. 'Hi, Rab. Good to see you. How's it going?'

'I'm doing fine, Cathie. Thanks to you. Met the new boss, Steve, yesterday. Nice guy. Fulham supporter. Started on a block of flats he's converting. Went well. All came back to me. Just like riding a bike.'

'So he was happy with your work?'

'Yeah. He checked it and said I did a good job.'

'That's great, Rab. And how's the flat?'

'Just perfect, Cathie. And the women in the other flats are friendly. Matter of fact, I took my next-door neighbour, Helen, out to a local pub last night.'

'Wow. Fast worker, huh? She single?'

'Yeah. A widow. Really nice, though.'

'You've done well for yourself, then?'

'Couldn't have done it without you, Cathie. How are *you* doing, hen? Anything I can do to help you?'

'Not at the moment. But sometimes I get unwanted attention from stray men. So I might call on you to help.'

'Any time, Cathie. Do anything for you and Alex.'

'You seem to have settled in fine. So we really don't need to meet like this. But Alex has money put aside. And he'll give you some if you need it.'

'I'm fine, Cathie. Get my wages next week and I'm off and running. But I'll call you if I need anything.'

'Okay. Let's swap numbers. Always call from a phone box. To avoid tracing. And don't use names.'

'I'll do that.'

'And if you ever get a tail, do you know the last-on last-off way of shaking it off?'

'No, I don't.'

'Okay. We'll go back to Hammersmith on the tube and I'll show you how to do it.'

***

Dmitri looked up as his secretary brought in the mail. He checked through it. A personal letter from London on the top. He recognised the handwriting. Jill Graham. Three weeks since he'd left London, and she'd told him it was over. What did she want now? He slit the envelope.

'Dear Dmitri,

Just a note to let you know I'm now leaving London. I've met someone else, and we're going back to my home town to start a new life there. So please don't try to contact me again. Jill'

No chance of that. He couldn't even remember her home town. In any case, he now wouldn't go back to UK for a long time. Nadya would cover for the next year.

His dad had organised his new ID using a specialist who worked for Deputy PM Beria. He had researched the family and came up with three options, all of whom were deceased distant cousins.

He had chosen Andrei Rykov, and the man was now creating the back story of his new secret name, which he'd use only in the UK. With a change in appearance, he hoped to get back to London after a year and pick up the threads of the UK business undetected. After all, the police hadn't even questioned Igor or Irina. Josh Calman reckoned Maxwell had no hard evidence on any of them. Fingers crossed.

Part 2
1948 / 1949

Chapter 12. Andrei Rykov

Dmitri stood under the tree and watched the entrance to the block of flats in South Kensington. The same spot he'd stood in twenty-one months ago to find the girl.

Since then, he'd become obsessed with her. In all his thirty-three years, he'd never physically hurt anyone. Except this girl. And he regretted it.

She had betrayed his cousin to the police, and so he chopped off the tip of her fourth finger on her right hand as punishment. But it weighed on his conscience. Guilt haunted him. And he needed to assuage it somehow. By being kind to her. Or generous, maybe. Without her knowing his true identity.

When he kidnapped her in 1946, she carried six IDs, and he didn't know which she used at the time. And his detective, Paul Lynch, didn't know either. Thought the police had put her into a witness protection programme with a new ID.

On his last visit in February, the first using his new ID, Dmitri had gone into the block of flats to check if her name appeared on the display board in the lobby.

Only Lorna Mitchell, in flat three, matched any of the six names on his list. He had then followed her one day as she strolled up to Hyde Park, round the lake, and did some shopping on her way back.

Now she'd appeared from the block again, and he followed at a discreet distance. Looked like the same route as before.

Last time, she had crossed the bridge, walked round the lake clockwise, and stopped at a bench half-way back on the south side to rest and admire the view across the lake and the park towards Marble Arch.

He decided to walk anti-clockwise along the south side and sit on the same bench. He bought a newspaper from a vendor, and sat reading it while watching her stroll along the far side in her pale blue dress, and white hat, shoes, gloves and handbag.

As she came along towards him, his stomach tensed. He needed to say something to get her to stop and talk.

He leaned back to enjoy the warm May sunshine, and as she passed said, 'Hi. Lovely day for a walk, huh?'

She stopped in surprise. 'Yes, it is.'

'May I say something else?'

'Go on.'

'Today, I had a surprise gap in my schedule. I'm sat here enjoying the sunshine and the view. And suddenly, you make it even lovelier. Thank you. Would you care to have a seat for a minute?'

She pursed her lips. 'Okay.' And sat beside him. 'You're clearly not British. No Brit would ever give a woman a compliment like that.'

He laughed. 'No. I'm Andrei from Kiev.' He held out his hand, and she shook it.

'I'm Lorna. Where's Kiev? Never heard of it.'

'In Ukraine. Do you know where that is?'

She shook her head. 'No.'

'Do you know where France is?'

'Yes. Across the English Channel.'

'Right. If you keep going east from France, you get to Germany. And the next country east is Poland. After that is Ukraine. And Kiev is its beautiful capital city. Like London.'

'Well, now I know. How often do you come here?'

'About every three months. My first visit here was in February. For business with British companies.'

'Wow. Your English is very good.'

'We study it at school and university.'

'So, what business are you in?'

'We work with your British companies to take some of their clever ideas back to Ukraine. What about you? What do you enjoy most?'

'Oh, reading, music, going to the cinema or theatre.'

'I like these too. Who's your favourite film star?'

'Ginger Rogers. She's brilliant.'

'I was just reading about her. She's in a new film.' He turned the paper over to the cinema page. 'Here you are. "It Had to Be You". Do you know that cinema?'

She looked at the paper. 'Yes, it's near Leicester Square. In the centre of London.'

'May I take you to see it? As a thank you for talking to me? I've enjoyed meeting you. We could have a meal before it, if you like?'

She glanced at him and smiled. 'Okay.'

'Good. Where do you live?'

'South Kensington.'

'Well, I'm in a hotel there. The Runcorn. Do you know it? Small, but high quality. I like it.'

'No, I don't know it.'

'Shall we walk and I'll show you where it is?'

'Okay. Let's do that.'

They strolled back towards his hotel. He kept the conversation light. Presented himself as an eager tourist, asking her questions about London. She seemed to enjoy his company.

'Here we are. This is my hotel. Do you live near?'

'Just five minutes away. That way.'

'I have a meeting this afternoon, but should be clear by five. Could we meet here at five-thirty? And do you like fish? I know a good fish restaurant in Soho.'

'Yes, I like fish. See you later, then.'

He watched her walk away. Paul Lynch had said she was a professional lure? He had to be careful.

***

Lorna walked back towards her flat and headed for the shops. He seemed a nice guy. The right type. An open, friendly businessman. Neatly trimmed moustache and beard. And she missed male company.

Two years ago, her brother, Alex, had landed a twelve-year sentence. A startling blow. And her married lover, Armin, whom she'd met ten years earlier, and with whom she'd made passionate love several times a week, had returned to Switzerland. He now only came to London once a month.

She needed to fill the gap. But not with just anyone. She attracted men wherever she went, because she kept her looks fresh and her figure trim. But with their first words either sleazebag or juvenile, they didn't last five seconds with her.

Andrei was different. Admired her, but with a nice, respectful approach. And she liked that. Let's see how it worked out later.

***

Dmitri stood in the hotel foyer and watched people and traffic passing outside. She arrived on the dot at five-thirty. Had now added a matching pale blue coat to her outfit. 'Hi, Lorna. You look great.'

'Oh, thank you. Are we ready to go?'

'Yes. I'll just get the desk to order a taxi.'

'Don't bother. Just take the tube. It's a lot easier.'

'Okay, then. Let's go.'

They strolled round to South Kensington station and caught the tube to Piccadilly Circus. He chatted about his day. Then up Shaftesbury Avenue and through to Wheeler's restaurant in Old Compton Street.

'I can recommend the Dover Sole here, Lorna. It's sensational. And a white Burgundy to go with it?'

'Okay, fine. I'll go along with that.'

He ordered and sat back. She still wore her gloves, and he wanted to see her finger.

'The cinema programme starts at eight, so we should have plenty of time. Tell me about yourself. Do you work or are you a lady of leisure?'

Just then, the waiter arrived with two small dishes. 'An amuse-bouche for you. Our version of a prawn cocktail. Please enjoy.' He placed a dish at each place.

She glanced over at him. 'What's this?'

'Just a small appetiser. To cleanse the palate.'

She took off her gloves and picked up the cutlery that came with the dish. He tensed as he saw her finger. Looked very neat, with skin folded over where he had cut off the tip so long ago. Felt guilty about it now.

The wine waiter opened the bottle and poured a sample into his glass. He tasted it and nodded, and the waiter filled their glasses.

He picked his up and smiled. 'Cheers.'

She smiled back. 'Cheers. And thank you.'

'My pleasure. Thank you for coming. My last night in London for a while. Back to Kiev tomorrow. Couldn't be with better company.'

'Oh? Kind of you to say so.'

'So, tell me about yourself.'

'Well, I had a job as secretary to one of the top men at the War Office during the war. But when it ended, I left. Not sure what to do now. Don't need to rush into anything, though. I have a small private income.'

'Oh? Nice.'

'Let's not exaggerate. My father died two years ago and left me a large house at a seaside resort in Scotland. The rental income allows me to live okay down here.'

'Sorry to hear that. I mean, about your father. But glad you live here now.' *No mention of a professional lure. And was it the truth?*

She smiled. 'Thanks. So, to answer your question, at the moment I'm a lady of leisure.'

He lifted his glass. 'Cheers to that. Forgive me. I notice your short finger. Was that an accident?'

She glanced at it. 'Yeah. Lost the tip in a bike chain as a kid. No big deal. Just means I can't play a piano.'

'Oh. Did you play the piano?'

'I meant it as a joke, Andrei.'

'Sorry. I don't always get British humour.'

'No problem.'

The waiter came with their main courses and he chatted about his childhood in Kiev. *But be wary. This woman could lie for England. Even used Sergei's story. How far did he want to go? She fascinated him, though. He wanted to go further if he could.*

They left the restaurant and headed for the cinema. Two hours later, they emerged and strolled towards Piccadilly Circus station. 'Did you like Ginger Rogers?'

She grimaced. 'Not really. Stupid story. But she's such a good actress, she just about made it believable. I loved her in Top Hat and Swing Time with Fred Astaire. Saw them a dozen times. She's just not the same now.'

'Oh, that's a shame.'

'No, no. I've enjoyed being with you.'

He smiled. 'That's okay, then.'

He got their tickets and they descended the escalator to the westbound platform. He moved to go further along the platform to get away from the crowd, but she said. 'No. Stay at this end. The exit at South Ken is just here. It saves a walk at that end.'

He walked her to her block of flats. *Would she invite him up for a coffee?* She held out her hand. 'Thank you very much, Andrei. I've really enjoyed tonight.'

No, she wouldn't. 'My pleasure, Lorna. May I see you again when I return at the end of August?'

'Yes, of course.' She gave him her number. 'Just give me a call when you arrive.'

'Thank you. See you then. *Udachi*.'

'What's that?'

'Oh, sorry. It's a family word. It kind of means best of luck or Godspeed.'

'Okay. See you.' She turned and opened the door.

***

She glanced round to make sure he'd left. Then dashed to the lift, got into her flat, and sat on the floor of her hall with her back against the door. Couldn't move. Couldn't breathe. Her head jangled. The same voice. The same word. It echoed the last time she'd heard it. The day he kidnapped her. In a taxi. He'd done that. No doubt. No bloody doubt. It still echoed in her head. The bastard. So nice. So genuine. So open. Even asked about her finger. The bastard. What did he want? Why do it? Some stupid sport? Guilt? Remorse? The bastard.

Half-an-hour later, she lifted her head off her knees, gave herself a shake, prepared a gin and tonic, and sat in her easy chair. Thoughts swirled around her head.

She woke next morning, still in her chair, and went to the bathroom to freshen up. An outline plan had formed, and she let it soak in during the morning.

In the afternoon, she set out what she had to do on paper. By five o'clock, she burned her notes, went out shopping, and stopped at a phone box near the station.

'Hi, it's me. I'd like to talk to you about how you could help me with something. Can we meet at Barons Court tube station tomorrow at one o'clock? There's a café just on your right as you exit the station. Do a couple of last-on, last off changes on the way.'

'Okay. Do anything for you. See you then.'

She hung up. First step of her plan in place.

***

Dmitri dumped his bags on the bed, picked up the phone, and asked for the number.

'Hi Lorna? It's Andrei from Kiev. Remember me?'

'Oh, hello Andrei. Of course. Back in London?'

'Yeah. Just got in. Back in the Runcorn. I know it's late, but I thought I'd call you and see if we could meet up tomorrow like we did before? You know, dinner at Wheelers and the cinema. What do you think?'

'Well, let me check my diary. Tomorrow. Thursday. Second September. Can I fit you in?' She paused. 'I'm clear. Just joking. I'd love to meet tomorrow. Will I come round to your hotel at five-thirty again?'

'Yes. I'll be clear by then. Look forward to seeing you, Lorna.'

'Me too.'

'Till tomorrow, then. Good night.'

'Good night.'

He hung up. She sounded so warm. So beautiful. He'd spent lots of time over the summer thinking about her. Here for a week, so maybe he could get closer to her over the weekend. Maybe another Jill? Fingers crossed.

Better prepare for tomorrow's meetings. Barclays International in the morning. Lunch with a professor at London University, and a discussion on his research.

Next day, he stood looking out from the hotel foyer and saw her approach on time. Salmon-pink coat and white hat, gloves, bag and shoes again. His heart leaped, and he dashed out to meet her.

'Wow. You look great, Lorna. Brilliant to see you again. Thank you so much.'

She smiled. 'Thank you. Good to see you too.'

All the way to the restaurant, they chatted about their summers. Just like old friends, he thought.

After the main course, he said, 'I've brought you a present. Hope you like it.'

As he went into his pocket, her eyes widened, and she smiled in anticipation. He gave her a little box.

She opened it and gasped. 'My God. It's beautiful.'

He watched her lift the brooch from the box and study it. A small gold butterfly with emerald body and diamond encrusted wings. 'It's my great-grandmother's passed down to me. I'd like to give it to you as a token of my admiration. Please accept it.'

She looked up. 'Andrei, I can't accept this. We don't really know each other. This is only our second date. You can't give away an heirloom like this.'

'I can. It's mine to do what I like with. And I want to give it to you. To enhance your beauty. That's it.'

She stared at him in silence. 'Okay, I accept it. Thank you so much.' She pinned the brooch to her lapel and put the box in her handbag. 'How does it look?'

'Beautiful. Just like you.'

She smiled. 'Thank you again.'

'You're welcome. Let's get to the cinema.'

She had chosen to see "Sorry, Wrong Number", and it was a real thriller. He enjoyed it too.

She hooked her arm in his as they strolled to the tube station and waited on the platform. The crowd surged in from the entrance behind them and spread along its length. He heard a train approaching in the tunnel.

A man poked him in the back. He freed himself from Lorna's arm and turned. 'Hey, watch it.'

'Yeah, mister moneybags. You ruined my family. Killed my dad.'

'I don't know what you're talking about.' He looked around. People were staring at him. Lorna looked in a panic. He stared at the man. Short, with a Cossack type hat, glasses and moustache. He'd never seen him before.

'Oh, you bloody do know. Borodin. You and your money ruined our lives.'

The man pushed him hard on the chest and shouted '*Udachi*'. He staggered back off the edge of the platform as the train roared in to the station. *Was that a flash of triumph in Lorna's eyes? How could she know …*

***

Lorna "fainted" on the platform, holding her handbag. The noise was horrendous. The train screeched to a halt. Steel wheels sliding on steel rails. Women screamed in hysterics. Men shouted. Someone checked her pulse. 'Can we get her on to that bench?'

Someone lifted her shoulders and someone else her legs and laid her flat. A man shouted over the tannoy, 'Please clear the platform. Clear the platform.'

She coughed and slowly opened her eyes. A face close to her. A woman. 'Are you okay?'

'Andrei? Where's Andrei?' She tried to lift her head.

'Just stay still for a moment. I'm a nurse.'

It sounded like chaos around her. Men shouting. Women screaming. The front part of the train at the platform with the doors closed and people trying to get off. She lay back with her eyes closed.

A few minutes later, a man said, 'Excuse me, ma'am. I'm from London Transport Police. Did you see what happened?'

The woman beside her said, 'Yes, I did.'

'Could you tell me, please? First, your name and address.'

She gave him the info and launched into her account of what happened. Lorna lay and listened. The woman told him. Very accurate. Very precise. *Very good.*

'Is this woman okay?'

'Yes, but I think she's in shock.'

Lorna opened her eyes. A man in uniform.

'Can you sit up, ma'am?'

She nodded and struggled to sit up. He helped her. 'I'm Sergeant Burns from London Transport Police. Can you tell me what happened?'

She struggled to speak. 'Where's Andrei?'

'Is that the man you were with?'

'Yes. What happened to him?'

The sergeant glanced at the woman beside him. 'I'm afraid he's dead, ma'am. Killed outright.' The woman leaned over and stroked her shoulder.

Lorna dropped her head. 'No. He can't be.'

'Can you give me his name, ma'am?'

She looked at him, puzzled. 'Andrei.'

'And his second name?'

'I don't know.'

'Can you tell me anything about him?'

'He's from Kiev. That's in Ukraine. Staying in a hotel in South Kensington.'

'Which hotel, ma'am?'

'Erm. The Runcorn.'

'Excuse me a sec.' He stood up and waved over another man in uniform. 'Danny. His name's Andrei something. From Kiev. Staying at the Runcorn in South Ken. Call the Met to get someone over to check on him.'

He sat again. 'What's your name, ma'am?'

'Lorna Mitchell.'

He took notes. 'And your address?'

She told him.

'And how do you know Andrei?'

'I don't, really. It's only the second time I've met him. I first met him three months ago. In Hyde Park. We chatted, and he invited me for dinner and the cinema. He seemed really nice, so I agreed. He then went back to Kiev the next day.

'Last night, he called me. Back in London for business. He invited me out again tonight for dinner and the cinema. We were just heading back to South Ken when this happened.'

'Can you tell me exactly what happened?'

'Well, we were just waiting for a train, and this man started shouting at Andrei. Told him he had used his money to ruin the man's family. And kill his father.'

'Did Andrei know this man?'

'No. He said he didn't know what the man was talking about. And then the man shouted, "You bastard", and pushed him off the platform.' She dropped her head again and covered her eyes.

'Can you describe this man?'

'Short. Stocky. Glasses. Moustache. Black coat. Black hat. But not an ordinary hat. There's a name for the type of hat. But I just can't remember it. Sorry.'

'How tall was the man?'

'Slightly shorter than me. Maybe five six?'

'And did he speak with an accent?'

'Yes, he did.'

'Did you recognise it?'

'No. Sounded kind of foreign.'

'Did you see where the man went?'

'I didn't. I was so shocked at Andrei falling off the platform. When I looked back, the man had gone.'

'Okay, ma'am. Thanks for that. I'll have one of my team escort you home in a car. We'll come tomorrow and check if you remember anything else.'

She struggled to her feet, and another policeman took her up to street level, and stayed with her until she entered her flat.

She poured herself a gin and tonic, and flopped into her easy chair. Mission complete.

Chapter 13. Sandra Maxwell Two

Sandra relished life in London. Confident at work and content at home. Last month, she'd celebrated two years in London. How time flies.

She'd halved her clear-up times, and Foreign Office involvement no longer extended them. Now with just a few outliers, both good and bad, but reasons known. And that included an increased workload from Interpol.

Dave Burnett's feedback at her annual reviews echoed her own feelings of success, and he'd applied much of her procedure changes in other Regions.

At home, Chuck also enjoyed life with BEA. Now a Senior Captain, he also had rave reviews. He'd now recovered that personal assurance and authority he had when she first knew him.

And together, they'd found a new delight in travel to foreign places. Chuck had access to concession fares, and when his shift pattern gave him four days off over a weekend, they often visited a European city. Sandra loved Paris, and had started to learn French.

For the last two years, they had spent their summer holiday in the US. She enjoyed meeting his daughter, Amy, and his extended family, and visiting New York City and Niagara Falls.

She'd also made friends with Olivia Fulwood, who lived two floors below her. They'd met in the lift one day and chatted as they went shopping.

Olivia was a widow a couple of years older than Sandra. Her husband had worked for the Foreign Office for years, but died a year ago from an illness he'd picked up in Khartoum. Olivia seemed well-connected and could get tickets for anything at short notice.

They went a few times to the Summer Olympics at the Empire Stadium at Wembley, and cheered all the athletes, including Fanny Blankers-Koen and Alice Coachman, winning their gold medals.

She and Chuck followed the US Basketball team as they won their gold medals. And formed a foursome with Olivia and her friend, Digby Barfield, a barrister, for Friday night drinks and dinner.

On Friday morning, she held her usual management meeting at nine. She still had her five Divisions, but had now appointed Barry to head up South-East Division as well as maintaining the clear-up times' analysis.

After the meeting, she and Brian Walker, her number two, sat on to discuss a complex case in his Central Division. Her phone rang. 'An Inspector Hastie from London Transport Police for you, ma'am.'

'Put him through.'

'CS Maxwell? I'd like to come and see you to discuss an incident at Piccadilly Circus station last night. A man pushed on to the tracks and killed.

'We've just got his prints check back, and it's a match for a Dmitri Petrov. A note on his file says we have to inform you of any match.'

'Wow. What ID did he have?''

'Andrei Rykov. A Russian national.'

'Please come round right away.'

'Will do, ma'am. I'd like to bring Inspector Todd from the Met. He's also involved in the case.'

'Yes, of course. See you in a few minutes.'

She turned to Brian. 'Need to call MI5.' She got connected. 'Eliot? Remember Dmitri Petrov?'

'The Russian from Victoria Point?'

'Yeah. Killed last night at Piccadilly Circus tube station. Someone pushed him on to the tracks. Carrying false ID. Got some cops coming round to tell us about it. Want to join us?'

'Be with you in ten minutes.' She hung up.

'Brian, could you get the Petrov file, please? This might blow open the whole Victoria Point case again.'

Ten minutes later, they all sat round Sandra's table, and she introduced everyone to Chris Hastie and Ray Todd. 'Right, Chris, tell us what happened.'

'Thanks, ma'am. At 22.32 last night, we attended an incident at Piccadilly Circus tube station. An incoming train on the westbound Piccadilly Line had killed a man pushed off the platform.

'He carried a Russian passport in the name Andrei Rykov, Director of Victoria Point Investments, with an address at Barclays International here in London. We passed his details to the Russian Embassy first thing this morning before we had the prints info.

'We took statements at the scene from three female witnesses, two independent and the man's companion. The best was an A&E nurse at Charing Cross Hospital. Clear and precise. Kept her head in a stressful situation.

'She said a man had poked another man in the back standing with a woman next to her and her husband. When the man turned, the poker shouted, "You and your money ruined our family and killed my father."

'The other man said he didn't know what he was talking about. And the man said, "You bloody do know. Borodin." Then shouted what sounded like, "You datched it", and pushed him off the platform. The incoming train hit him full on.

'She described the attacker as short, about five foot six, and with a stocky build. Wore a black Cossack hat, glasses and moustache. Black gloves and coat. Spoke with a foreign accent. The whole thing lasted only a few seconds. She didn't see the attacker leave, and assumed he'd gone via the entrance beside them.

'The other two witnesses added nothing, except the man's companion said she thought he shouted, "You bastard" as he pushed. But the nurse thought her words were more accurate.

'Our team searched the station, but could find no other witnesses of the attacker. They did, however, find a paper bag with glasses and a false moustache stuffed in a litter bin near the Bakerloo Line platforms. So he may have used one of these trains to leave. No prints off the glasses, ma'am.

'The companion gave us details of the dead man's hotel, and we asked the Met to check there. So, I'll pass over to Ray for the rest.'

Sandra said, 'Thanks, Chris. Got a photo of him?'

He pulled a photo from his file and passed it over.

She compared it with Petrov's photo from her file. 'Beard and moustache really change his appearance, huh? Okay, go ahead, Ray.'

'Right, ma'am. At Chris's request, we attended at the Runcorn Hotel in South Kensington. Mr Rykov had checked-in on Wednesday night. He made one phone call to his female companion, obviously setting up the date for the following evening.

'We've studied his diary and notebook. His scheduled business meetings were Thursday at Barclays and London University; Friday in Cambridge at a company called CCM Ltd; Monday in Oxford at a company called BE Ltd; Tuesday in Southampton at UCS; and Wednesday at Barclays again.

'So far, all these check out as genuine business contacts. We assume he'd spend the weekend with his girlfriend. His itinerary showed travel from Moscow to Warsaw to London on the Wednesday, and the return journey the following Wednesday. We can find nothing suspicious about his movements or contacts.

'However, with his prints matching this Russian, Dmitri Petrov, and your involvement, ma'am, we'll need to recheck him. We think this incident has all the hallmarks of a Russian on Russian hit.'

'Oh, really? Why do you say that, Ray?'

'Well, ma'am. We have a very active Russian community in north London. Lots of political enemies and mafia-like action. Lots of violence, including murders. Seems the most likely cause here.'

'Mmm. Let's not rush to conclusions at this stage. In a Russian on Russian hit, we'd expect them to talk in Russian. But according to Chris, they spoke English.'

Ray pursed his lips and glanced at Chris.

She went on. 'So, going further. Did they speak English because their business dispute happened here? Or maybe in another European country where they used English as a common language? But I think we should start looking here.' She glanced at Eliot. 'Gives us a chance to look at their books again? What do you think?'

Eliot nodded.

Ray coughed. 'Can I ask why MI5 is here?'

'You can. But I can't give you an answer.'

Sandra cut in. 'Okay. Let's work out how we should take this forward.'

Ray interrupted. 'With respect, ma'am, I think there are too many cooks in this broth. I'll withdraw and pass all the info we've gathered to you.'

'Fine. Will you clear that decision with your boss?'

'Will do, ma'am. Thank you.' He left the room.

'Okay, let's get back to what we should do. On the face of it, a business deal has gone sour. And it must be one that VPI cancelled. So let's act on the evidence and raid their premises here in London. Let's see if we can identify the link between these two men. You happy with that, Chris?'

'Yes, ma'am.'

'What else do we need to do? What about the man's female companion? Do we need to interview her?'

'No, ma'am. She's a genuine, innocent bystander. Met him by chance three months ago for the first time. This was her second date. Fainted at the scene and took time to recover.'

'Known to us at all?'

'We checked, ma'am. Not known. Scottish girl. Speaks like you.'

'Oh? What's her name?'

'Lorna Mitchell, ma'am.'

Sandra dropped her pen. 'Very attractive, with a flat in South Kensington?'

'Yes, ma'am.' He read out the address.

'I can tell you right now, Chris. Your case has just become way more complex. Genuine and innocent don't apply to her in any sense. We know her very well. And that gives us another angle to check. Did she set it up?'

'I find that hard to believe, ma'am. Our nurse witness checked her at the scene. She displayed all the symptoms of shock. Rapid breathing and pulse. I'd have staked my pension she was genuine. If she's not, she must be a hell of an actress.'

'That she is. I won't give you details on why it's necessary, but I will check her out. However, I'll keep your view in mind.'

'Thank you, ma'am.'

'Right. Brian, let's get a search warrant for the Hanover Terrace property. My authority. Bring in all papers relating to Victoria Point Investments. And bring in the girl. That should be interesting.'

'What about the Dubovs ma'am?'

'Yeah. Bring in Igor. He might know something.'

Brian left the room.

Chris stood. 'I'll let you get on with it, ma'am. Just keep me informed.' He also left the room.

Sandra shook her head and smiled at Eliot. 'Can you believe it? A golden chance to see their finances again. Do you have your own forensic accountants?'

'Yeah, we do. We'll work alongside you on that. I'll report back, and return when you've got the stuff here.'

'Why didn't we know he was here, Eliot?'

'Well, when this whole thing blew up a couple of years ago, the only Petrov contact we knew about was Professor James Cawthorne in Cambridge.

'We went to see him and asked him to let us know in secret if Petrov returned. But he never did. We checked with him last year. He told us that Petrov's sister had visited him. But he thought we only wanted to know when Petrov himself came over.

'Some of our guys suspect foreign spies everywhere in Cambridge. Lots of rabid communists there in the thirties. So we checked him out. But he came up clean. And Rykov didn't schedule a meeting with him.

'I think Cawthorne's just a bit scatter-brained. Maybe we didn't make it clear enough what we wanted.'

'Okay. See you later. It'll be an interesting day.'

She checked her notes. Why would the nurse witness say the man shouted, "You datched it", while Lorna said he shouted, "You bastard"? If he'd said the latter, the nurse would surely have caught that no problem.

She then checked the Petrov file and saw that Lorna had said, when they kidnapped her, the 'doctor' had shouted to the taxi driver, "You dash" or something like it. She assumed the 'doctor' was Petrov.

If Ray was right, and it was a Russian on Russian hit, did these two men use the same Russian word?

She called the Berlitz School, where she took French lessons, and spoke to one of the Russian tutors. She explained she was looking for a Russian word that sounded like "You dash" or "You datched it".

'Well, ma'am, I think the word you may be looking for is "Udachi". She spelt it out. It's used by people from the Moscow area as a farewell greeting, like "Best of luck" or "Godspeed".'

'Thank you so much. Bye'.

Exactly the right word. She'd talk to Lorna about it later. Maybe Russian on Russian was right?

***

Lorna smiled at Sandra. 'Nice to see you too, ma'am, but why am I here?'

'As Brian told you, to help with our enquiries into the incident at Piccadilly Circus station last night.'

'Oh, right? Well, I'm happy to help if I can.'

'How well did you know Andrei Rykov?'

'Not well at all. That was only our second meeting.'

'How did you first meet him?'

I take regular daytime walks up to Hyde Park and listen to a band or walk round the lake. One day last May, I walked along the lake side, and as I passed him sitting on a bench, he spoke to me.'

'Had you seen him before?'

'No, never. He was very polite. Very charming. And invited me to sit and chat for a moment. He told me he'd come from Kiev, Ukraine, on business. We chatted for about ten minutes, then walked back to South Ken.

'He invited me out to dinner and the cinema that evening. He seemed an open, friendly businessman, and I don't have a man in my life at present. So I agreed.'

'Did you think it might lead somewhere?'

'Yeah. Possibly. He was my type.'

'And what then?'

'We met later. He took me to dinner at Wheelers in Soho, and then the cinema to see a Ginger Rogers film. Then back home. Very enjoyable evening.'

'Back to your flat?'

'No, no. Don't go that far on a first date. We parted at the entrance. But I agreed to see him again next visit. He flew back to Kiev next day.

'He then called me on Wednesday. Just arrived and invited me to repeat the date on Thursday. So, I agreed and looked forward to it.

'We had a good time. At dinner, he gave me a gift as a token of his admiration. I've still got it here.' She went into her handbag and passed over a small box. 'He said it belonged to his great-grandmother. I was gobsmacked.'

Sandra opened the box and saw the golden brooch. 'My God, that's beautiful. What a gift.' *What was this guy doing? Why give such a gift to the woman he'd maimed? Guilt complex perhaps? And maybe she didn't know his real ID?*

'It sure is.'

'Did he tell you anything about his business?'

'Just that he came over here to take clever British ideas back to Kiev. That's all he said.'

'Mmm. Did he ever ask about your finger?'

'What? No!' She glanced down at her right hand. 'He was far too polite to do that.'

'His diary showed he had a free weekend. Do you think he planned to spend it with you?'

'Yeah. Probably. We got on well together.'

'Okay. Can we talk about the events at the tube station? Just tell me what you saw.'

She related the incident just as she had told the LT police officer, and it matched the statement from the nurse witness except for the shouted comment.

'You say the man shouted, "You bastard". Are you sure about that?'

Well, I think so. I was in panic mode by then.'

'Could it have been "Udachi"?'

She raised her eyebrows. 'Suppose it could.'

'Have you ever heard that word before?'

She looked puzzled. 'No, never.'

Sandra picked up the Petrov file and opened it. You said when the man kidnapped you two years ago, he shouted to the taxi driver, "You dash, or something like it". Could it have been that word, "Udachi"?'

'Suppose so. I don't remember that. What does it mean, anyway?'

'It's a Russian word meaning "Best of luck" or "Godspeed". A farewell greeting.'

'So, does that mean the attacker was Russian?'

'Had you ever seen that man before?'

'What? Why would you ask that? I don't know any Russians. And I've never seen him.'

'Okay. I have to tell you Andrei Rykov was Russian. Not Ukrainian. Worked for the same company as the man who kidnapped you and cut off your finger.'

'What?' She stared back. 'Is there a link?'

'Well, what do you think?'

'I don't know. Never saw the man who kidnapped me. But if Andrei's a mate, he must have got my details from the kidnapper and set out to meet me. Creepy. Yet he seemed genuine. Gave me that beautiful gift.'

'Maybe an attempt to make you think better of Russians? We know the kidnapper left this country the day after he maimed you, and never returned. This man then did the same job. His passport tells us he came here in February and May this year, before his recent visit.'

'So, do you think Andrei knew the kidnapper had maimed me? He wanted to take a different approach? More genuine? Hence the gift?'

'Maybe. But I want to catch his killer.'

'Is he another Russian?'

'Don't know yet.'

'Oh. Just thought. If he used Russian words. So, is there anything else I can do?'

'No. You've been very helpful, thanks. Let's leave it there. Your car's waiting. But if you're approached by any more Russians, it's worth letting me know.'

'Okay. Will do. Bye.'

Sandra watched her go. *Cool customer. No evidence she was involved, though. Innocent reaction to 'Udachi' and no indication she thought Andrei was Dmitri. No suspicious manner. But asked twice whether the attacker was Russian? Why did she want to know that? Was she that good an actress? Possibly. Still not sure. Let's put a tail on her and tap her phone. Just in case.*

***

Sandra and Brian sat opposite Igor Dubov and his pushy lawyer from Josh Calman's practice. 'We demand to know, ma'am, why you've brought Mr Dubov here. Is he under arrest?'

'No, he's not. He's here to help with our enquiries.'

'Into what?'

'An incident at Piccadilly Circus tube station last night. Just calm down and let me explain.'

'Oh, sorry, ma'am.'

'Last night, a man was pushed on to the tracks and killed by an incoming train. He carried ID in the name, Andrei Rykov. A Russian national.'

At the mention of the name, Dubov sat up straight and stared at her. 'Andrei? Killed? No. Can't be.'

'I'm afraid it's true. Another man attacked him. Short and stocky. Said Andrei had ruined the man's family and killed his father. As you know, Mr Rykov was a Director of VP Investments. Hence why we've brought in all relevant documents to help identify this attacker. Do you know anyone that fits that description?'

'No. I know no one like that. VPI has good clients. With no problems.'

174

The lawyer cut in. 'You've no right to grab these papers without a warrant. They're confidential.'

Sandra glanced over. 'We have a warrant. Now, Mr Dubov. The man shouted a Russian word as he pushed Andrei. Udachi. Does that mean anything to you?'

'Andrei and his family used that word every time they leave someone. Means best of luck. So it must be someone that knows him. Was he Russian?'

'We're told he spoke English with a foreign accent. Do you know a Russian who could be this man?'

'No. No one. I don't know who would do this.'

'Do you have problems with any clients?'

'I don't know details. I manage properties. But don't manage any investment business. Sorry.'

She'd get nothing else useful here. And she didn't want to reveal she knew Rykov's real ID. 'Okay, let's leave it at that for the moment. Would you accompany my colleague to identify the body, please?'

'Yes, I will do that.'

'Thank you. We appreciate your help.'

'You're welcome.'

Sandra stood. 'If you think of anything else that may help us, please call me.' She gave Dubov a card.

So, what would happen when the news got back to Moscow? Lenkov at the Embassy would again have the whole Petrov family on his back. Good luck with that. She'd expect his call in a few days.

***

By Wednesday of the following week, Barry had added the murder of Dmitri Petrov, aka Andrei Rykov, to the list of active cases. But they still had no leads.

Back in her office, Sandra's phone rang. 'Inspector Chris Hastie, ma'am.'

'Good morning, Chris. Got some news?'

'I do, ma'am. Just had the forensics report on our victim's clothing. The nurse witness said the attacker poked the victim in the back. So they checked his coat.

'They found micro fibres of black knit wool gloves. The type sold by large stores like M&S.

'They also found traces of plumbers putty on these fibres. It's a unique blend of powdered clay and linseed oil transferred from fingers. They conclude the attacker's a plumber. If Ray's right, a Russian plumber. How many Russian plumbers do we have over here, ma'am? Very few, I'd guess.'

'Indeed. Thanks, Chris. I'll get right on it.'

She had a scheduled meeting in ten minutes with MI5 and the accountants, so called Brian.

She gave him the feedback. 'Let's start the trawl of Russians again. Try to find a Russian plumber this time. Five foot six tall, stocky build, and no confirmed alibi for last Thursday at 22.30.'

***

Sandra sat at her conference table with Eliot Forbes from MI5, Clive Semple, who led the team of forensic accountants, and her boss, Dave Burnett. 'Right, Clive. What have you found?'

'Since we last looked two years ago, Victoria Point Investments has added another offshore company to its group in the "Closed" part. Called VPI4. It sends thirty pounds a month to another offshore company, ML4.

'The other VPI companies, 1, 2, and 3, still send twenty pounds a month to their ML opposites. But VPI1 sent a one-off payment of two hundred pounds in May last year and this year. Maybe a bonus?

'The "Open" part, the main VPI company, still makes big profits. But two of its four post-war projects have now gone.

'They've retained a twenty-four percent stake in CCM Ltd of Cambridge, and in BE Ltd in Oxford. Both these have grown over the last two years.

'So, our targets for a business deal going sour rest with the two failed post-war projects. And we have no info on these. They've removed these paper trails back to the British Virgin Islands or maybe to Moscow.

'Now, I would think the owners in Moscow would provide that info if it helped bring their Director's killer to justice. But you'd have to check that yourself.

'We've gone as far as we can for the moment, but if you do get that info, we can check it for you. Sorry we can't give you the details you need today.'

'Well, thanks for your help, Clive. We'll get back to you if we get that info.'

He left the room.

Eliot leaned back. 'You know, he's right about these paper trails. It's a right bugger for us. You have to have the bit of paper for each step to find the path of a money trail. But that might change.

'One of our tech boffins went up to Manchester a few weeks ago. Saw a new electronic calculating machine called the Manchester Baby computer. About the size of this room. You can program it, and get answers to complex problems in just a few minutes.

'The machine can process calculations at eleven hundred per second. The next version will at least double that. Incredible.

'They think banks, insurance companies, etc, who process huge amounts of data manually, could use these computers to automate the process.'

Dave cut in. 'What happens to all the people who do the number crunching at the moment?'

'Well, in theory, the now more efficient company expands into new areas and retains them.

'But for us, you can see the benefits of linking these computers. It gives us electronic tracking. Kind of like how we can now track telephone calls.'

'How long will that take to achieve?'

'Years probably. But it's the way we're going. The march of technology.'

'Very interesting, Eliot. But can you give us an update on Mr B and his happy gang of spies?'

'Yes, of course. We've now tracked them for about two years. Intrigued by this new ML4 company, though. It might mean we have another spy in the ring that we don't know about. And that's a worry.

'We also know someone somewhere runs this ring. But we can't find him. So, what we've done is try to handle them as best we can until we do.

'Mr B and his girlfriend work in the Records Department at Portland. They're non-technical. So we no longer store our super-sensitive stuff there. And we have a small team which makes up a series of false but plausible records that will keep the Russians interested but lead them nowhere special.

'But that can't last forever. They'll get suspicious at some stage. It's a clever balance.'

'Sounds good. So, is there anything else you need from us today?'

'No, no, we're fine. Thank you both. Please keep me up to date with progress.' He left the room.

Sandra leaned forward. 'Got a dilemma, sir.'

'About what?'

'Clive made a good point about the two failed post-war projects. They're the obvious place to look for clues. But it might also be a business deal gone sour elsewhere in Europe, or even in Russia. And we can't yet rule out the girl. Lorna.

'Now, Chris contacted the Russian Embassy last Friday. By now they might know Rykov had a false passport, depending on how good it is. What do they do? The Petrovs are very powerful.

'Meanwhile, the Petrov family in Moscow would know last Friday from Igor Dubov, that Dmitri, aka Andrei Rykov, is dead. So, what do they do? If they contact Lenkov, the Chief at the Russian Embassy here, they have to use the Andrei Rykov ID. And I think that gives them a problem.

'Now, I haven't revealed to any of them that we know Rykov's real ID. And I'd like to keep it like that for a while longer. But we know from two years ago that a Russian bank owns VPI.

'So, I'm thinking about calling Lenkov to tell him someone killed Andrei Rykov last week. The Director of a Russian company. And we would like the owners to release details of the two failed UK projects so we can fully investigate the death. Force them to face the false ID. What do you think, sir?'

'Mmm. I think your instincts are sound, Sandra. Call Lenkov. Play it straight. It's what we'd do, anyway. And let's hope it breaks the log-jam, and allows us to move forward, one way or another.'

***

'Hello, Mr Lenkov. This is CS Sandra Maxwell here. We met two years ago to discuss your two Russians that the US had extradited from the UK?'

'Of course, ma'am. Do we have another problem?'

'Well, we might have. I'd like your help, please.'

'I'm happy to help, if I can.'

'Good. Let me explain. Last Thursday evening, a man attacked and killed another man at Piccadilly Circus tube station. He pushed him on to the tracks as a train arrived. The dead man carried a Russian passport in the name, Andrei Rykov. Do you know this name?'

'I do. London Transport Police told us on Friday. Since then we've tried to get more details. We want to repatriate the body. But they've not replied.'

'Do you know Rykov worked for a Russian-owned UK company called Victoria Point Investments? Evidence suggests revenge for a business deal gone sour. But the attacker fled, and we've no trace of him.

'We got a warrant to raid the company premises to find information that might help us identify him. We've now analysed this info. But we find that data on two recent failed projects is not available here.

'Now, a Russian bank owns this company. Therefore we'd like your help to get them to release this data. Have the owners already contacted you about this crime?'

'No. And I didn't make that link. Leave it with me, ma'am. I'll see what I can do.'

Sandra reported back to her boss. 'Lenkov didn't make the link to the Petrov's bank. And they in turn haven't contacted him. Even though they've known about it for several days.

'Of course, they might use a private detective like they did before. Good luck with that. I'll get an alert from LT Police if they hear anything.'

'Okay, good. I'd better let Hammond know at the Foreign Office, in case we have another diplomatic incident. What are we doing about the girl?'

'I've got a tap on her phone and a team tailing her. But it's a long shot. The only reason we're doing that is because we know her. On the face of it, she's an innocent bystander.'

'Fine. Keep me in the picture, Sandra.'

'Will do, sir.'

She went back to her office and thought about the situation. *Yet another complex case of false identities and multiple moving parts. How long to clear this?*

Chapter 14. Nadya Petrov

Nadya marched up the garden path, paused at the front door, took a deep breath, crossed her fingers for a sec, then pressed the doorbell. A few moments later, the door opened and a man with greying hair, bright eyes and a large warm smile greeted her. 'Nadya? You made it then? Come in. Come in. Good to meet you.'

'Thank you, Mr Lynch. Nice to meet you too.' She stepped inside and he closed the door behind her. 'As I said on the phone, you did a good job for us before, and I'd like to talk about another job.'

'That's fine. Let's go through to my office. And just call me Paul. We're not formal here.'

They settled on two easy chairs facing out to the garden, with a low table in front of them. He took a pad and pencil onto his lap.

'You want to talk about Dmitri? I liked him a lot. How is he these days?'

She swallowed and tried to keep calm. Couldn't get used to the loss of her brother. 'Someone killed Dmitri three weeks ago. Here in London. We want you to find out who and why, so we can get justice.'

'Oh, my God. So sorry for your loss. Of course I'll help in any way I can. Tell me about it.'

'Thank you. Can I have a glass of water, please?'

'Of course you can.' He leaned forward to the table, lifted a carafe, poured some water into a glass, and handed it to her. 'Just take your time, Nadya.'

'Dmitri was out on a date with a local woman. As they waited at Piccadilly Circus tube station, a man came up to them, shouted at Dmitri, and pushed him off the platform into the path of an incoming train.

'I have a police report here. Written again by Sandra Maxwell. It gives their view of the facts. But no firm conclusions. Just take a moment to read it.'

He read it twice. 'She describes what happened to an Andrei Rykov. A Russian national. Do I take it that Dmitri had this false ID? And do the police know that?'

'We don't think they do. Let me explain. It goes back two years to when you investigated what happened to two Russians.'

'Yeah. Remember it well. Held in the US.'

'Right. Can we agree this chat is confidential?'

'Absolutely. No question,'

'Okay. One of these men was my cousin Sergei. And at the time, Lenkov at the Embassy here pussy-footed around getting nowhere.

'Now, my father has a powerful position in Moscow. And he wanted action. He sent Dmitri over here to hire a good PD to find out what happened. And that's where you came in.

'You found out they were in the US. We knew we needed a swap to get them back. So Dmitri kidnapped two Americans, bypassed Lenkov, contacted Maxwell direct and made an offer they couldn't refuse. The swap took place a week later.

'Meanwhile, the police pulled in every Russian link they could find looking for the kidnappers. In fact, Dmitri told me much later the police interviewed him during this round-up. But he had a rock-solid alibi for the times of the kidnappings.'

'How did they get to him?'

'Well, when he visited here, unknown to us he stayed with a local woman called Jill Graham. A long-standing affair, which we kept from my father. He thinks a friend of hers, the wife of a cop, visited her flat one day and saw a couple of vodka bottles Dmitri had brought over. Showed a Russian link.'

'How about his alibis? Did they stand up?'

'He thinks so. They depended on him taking certain trains to and from Cambridge that day. He still had his tickets as part of an expenses claim and showed them as proof. They weren't time stamped or anything, but the police took photos of them.

'Dmitri left London the day after the swap. He claims he cleaned all the hard surfaces he'd touched. But a few days later, the police raided the girl's flat and the registered address of Victoria Point Investments, our UK company. So we think they might have found evidence somewhere that pointed to him.

'We couldn't take any chances with future visits, so I did some visits last year, while we established his new identity, Andrei Rykov, as a Director of VPI.'

'So, what happened this year?'

'For certain critical business reasons, we needed Dmitri across here again. He came over in February for a few days with a new appearance and the new ID. All went well. Then he came back again in May, and again all went well. But when he returned three weeks ago, it all went wrong. We need to find out why.'

'Well, I'll try. The police report eyewitnesses saying the attacker used "Borodin" and "Udachi", words that suggest a Russian on Russian attack. Is that possible?'

'We don't think so. We don't have any links to a family called Borodin. Either in business or otherwise. And our family use "Udachi" as a regular farewell greeting, as do many others. So, anyone who knew Dmitri could have used that word cynically.'

'Yes, he used it with me, Are you saying the attacker knew Dmitri?'

'No. We're saying the person who *organised* the attack knew Dmitri. And the other reason we don't think it was a Russian on Russian hit is they would have spoken Russian. And they spoke English.'

'Okay. Well, I'll start at the tube station and see how far we get. I try to avoid the police. They don't take kindly to PDs poking their noses into their business. But they also suggest a business deal gone sour as a reason. Is that possible?'

'Right. Let me explain why the police say that.' She explained the VPI company and its investments in the UK, and that the police had examined available records on their business dealings. 'They've asked us, via the Russian Embassy, to provide details of our two recent business failures here in the UK as the most likely sources to identify the attacker.

'So last week we re-examined these two projects ourselves. We know a hundred percent that neither is relevant. In each case, our University partners closed them for good technical reasons, with no animosity or problems with project staff. We've now fed that back via the London Embassy.

'Therefore, we've now concluded the true reason for the attack lay in Dmitri's personal life. Even though he had a wife and family in Moscow, we believe he was a bit of a ladies' man when he travelled.

'We found two telephone numbers in his papers, which we think were female contacts over here. And we would like you to focus your attention on them. These are the numbers.' She passed them over.

'Now, in addition, one night in June, I had to go to the office late one night to get something for my father. I found Dmitri sitting at his desk in tears, looking at a photo. He hid it in his desk and wouldn't talk about it. He'd drunk way too much vodka that night.

'I've now forced open his desk and retrieved that photo. Do you know who she is?'

He glanced at the photo. 'I don't know her name, but I know who she is. I took that photo and gave it to him.'

'What? How did that happen?'

He explained how, during the investigation for Dmitri two years ago, he'd identified the girl as a professional lure. Part of the gang that included the two Russians. And concluded she had betrayed the gang, and that was how the police caught them. The police had then put her in a witness protection programme.

He'd told Dmitri about her and took him to the block of flats where she lived. And that was the last time he saw Dmitri. He checked his old diary. 'That was on September 16, 1946.'

She checked her notes. 'Well, that's interesting. Let me tell you what happened that day.

'I spent part of yesterday grilling our UK property managers about this girl. I sensed they recognised her when I showed them the photo. To avoid me firing them, they admitted Dmitri had drugged and kidnapped the girl on that same date two years ago, brought her to one of our houses in the taxi we used, and chopped off the top of her fourth finger on her right hand as punishment.

'They said Dmitri seemed high that day. Might even have been on drugs himself. Then later, they loaded the girl and the remaining American into the taxi and dumped them in a side street behind Selfridges. The girl saw none of them. She was unconscious when they loaded her into the taxi and remained so throughout.

'Dmitri flew out the next day, and they cleared up all traces of visitors, and burned the blood-stained chopping board on a fire in the garden. The police raided the house a few days later and arrested them. But could find no evidence and let them go.'

'So why was Dmitri in tears over her photo?'

'Don't know. He wouldn't talk about it. But I've never known Dmitri to harm anyone or anything in his life. So maybe it was a guilty conscience.'

'Okay. I think you're right. Let me check both women out and get back to you.'

'What about payment?'

He gave her a flyer. 'That outlines our costs. When we worked for Dmitri, he paid in advance.'

'Right. I'll do the same. How much?'

'If I have to put a tail on them, it racks up costs. How about fifty? That should last up to five weeks. I'll give you a weekly report on progress and pay you back any excess. Happy with that?'

'Yes. Very happy. I'll give you my number in Moscow. It takes a few minutes to connect, but works okay.' She wrote out the number.

'Good. Here's a receipt. Look forward to working with you.'

She stood and shook hands. 'Me too.'

***

A week later, back in Moscow at her desk, with the fabulous domes of St Basil's Cathedral in the distance, Nadya's phone rang.

'A Mr Paul Lynch from London, madam.'

'Put him through.' The line connected. 'Hello. Paul, how are you today? A fine Monday here.'

'Here too, Nadya. Just to give you an update on last week. Think we've made some good progress.'

'Okay. Go ahead.'

'First, I went to the tube station. With the help of a few fivers to lubricate memories, I found the supervisor on platform duty the night of the attack.

'He didn't actually see the incident. At the time, he was further along the platform on the Tannoy system, asking people to move down the platform.

'As the train roared into the station, he heard screams and the screech of the emergency brakes as it came to a halt. He followed procedure, and got on the phone to call the police and get other staff to help.

'They cleared the platform of everyone other than eyewitnesses, blocked off access, and advised travellers to find alternate routes, before London Transport Police arrived to take control.

'The train driver sat frozen at his controls in shock, with tears flowing down his face. He got him to open his driver's door and tried to calm him down.

'He then went to help a girl who'd fainted. The companion of the man pushed on to the tracks. People had lifted the girl on to a nearby bench. Another woman knelt over her, and helped her recover.

'The other woman, an emergency nurse at Charing Cross Hospital, stayed with the girl until the police arrived and gave a detailed witness statement.

'The next day I found her at the hospital, and she told me what happened. The police report we read pretty much repeated her statement.

'Neither the supervisor nor the nurse could give me details of the girl. So I moved on and called the two numbers you gave me. I explained the death of Andrei Rykov, and that his family had retained me to find some details. I'd like to know their link to him.

'The girl at the first number, a flat at King's Cross, told me she had no link to any Russians and had no calls. But she had bought the flat over a year ago from her friend, Jill Graham, who had a Russian boyfriend. So maybe that was the connection?

'Jill had remarried, moved back to her home town, over two hundred miles away, and severed all her links with London. But she'd kept in touch with her, and gave me her number.

'So I called Jill. She hid nothing. Told me she didn't know Andrei, nor had heard from him. But she'd had a long relationship with a Russian man, Dmitri Petrov. She knew he had a wife and family in Moscow, but enjoyed his company when he was over here.

'But it had shocked her when police questioned her and him about his movements in September 1946. A few days later, after he had gone back home, they raided her flat, looking for him. She didn't know why, and they wouldn't tell her. So she told him she didn't want to see him again. And that was it. Never heard from him again.

'Shortly after, she met her husband on a blind date, and found they both wanted out of London. He's now a cop in Torquay, and she manages her parents' hotel.

'I explained Andrei worked for the same company as Dmitri, so maybe that was the link. But she said she wasn't interested, and we left it at that.

'I'm a hundred percent certain she has no link to Andrei's death.'

'Yeah. Sounds like it, Paul. What about the other number? Did that lead anywhere?'

'It sure did, Nadya. Straight to the girl in the picture. Andrei's companion on the fateful night.'

'Really? Wow! How did that go?'

'Well, let me tell you what I know. Then what I *think* I know. Then what I don't know.'

'Okay. Go ahead.'

'We met in a café near her flat. She said she'd like to talk about Andrei if it helped his family.

'She described her first chance meeting with him in May. As she walked in Hyde Park, he spoke to her from a bench, and they chatted. They then strolled back to his hotel, and he invited her to dinner and the cinema later.

'She enjoyed the date. Thought him a real nice guy. A very pleasant businessman from Kiev, and she agreed to see him again on his next visit.'

'Kiev? Why would he say that?'

'Maybe didn't want her to know he was Russian?'

'Mmm. Do you think they were intimate?'

'Oh, she didn't say, Nadya. But I don't think so. He left her at the entrance to her block of flats.'

'Okay. Sorry to interrupt.'

'He called her again on Wednesday the first, when he got back to London. She agreed to a repeat date the next night.

'Again, it was a perfect evening. Over dinner, he gave her a beautiful brooch as a token of his admiration. Said it had passed to him from his great-grandmother. She showed me it. Magnificent. A gold butterfly with emeralds and diamonds.'

'What? Could you hold on a sec? I need to check something next door.' She dashed through to Dmitri's office and opened his safe. The brooch had gone. *What the hell had he done? Such a valuable jewel?* She closed the safe, returned to her office, and picked up the phone. 'I'm so shocked, Paul. It's gone from here. Why would he do that? What possessed him to give her that precious heirloom? I can't believe it.'

'You're not the only one. Lorna couldn't believe it either. In fact, she refused it at first. But he insisted.'

'Lorna? Is that her name? What's her address? I'll look her up the next time I'm over.'

'Yeah. Lorna Mitchell.' He gave her the address. 'The reason? A guilty conscience, perhaps?'

'Maybe. Okay, let's press on.'

'Right. Of course, the perfect evening came to a sudden halt in the tube station. As they waited for a train, a man poked Andrei and shouted he had ruined his family and killed his father. And then pushed Andrei off the platform, and disappeared.

'Lorna fainted and was brought round by an off-duty nurse. Then the police took her home, and interviewed her the following day. That Sandra Maxwell woman. To get details of the attack at first hand. She said Maxwell focused on a Russian connection, quoting the words "Borodin" and "Udachi" the attacker used.

'But, other than that, she's had no further contact with the police. At this stage, I don't think she's part of it, Nadya. Other than as an innocent bystander.

'But you said the person behind this attack had to come from his personal life rather than his business life. You still sure about that?'

She hesitated. *They had only examined the contacts on the open part of their VPI business, and concluded they were not involved. But what about the secret part? Could that be involved? Their only link on that side was one of Beria's secret agents hidden deep in the Embassy in London. And he would leak nothing.* 'Yes, I'm sure. It has to be personal.'

'Yeah, that's what I thought. So, I put a tail on her. Just to see what happened. Now, that's what I know. Can I move on to what I *think* I know?'

'Yes, of course. Go ahead.'

'My tail on her is a mature couple. On Saturday morning, they called me. They had parked about fifty yards from her block of flats, and noticed two men in a car with a radio aerial parked five ahead.

'Looked like cops and wondered if they were also tailing Lorna. So I went down to join them.

'While we talked in our car, the two men left their car and walked in different directions. Within a minute, Lorna appeared, and headed for the tube station. Now, that told me the police must have a tap on her phone, and had alerted their men she was leaving.

'It also means, by the way, they knew I called her, and probably watched our meeting in the café. Maybe have a tap on my phone too. That's why I'm calling you from a colleague's phone.

'Anyway, we kept well back, and the two men followed her. She left the train at Holborn, and walked to the eastbound Central Line. She got on a train. The two cops and my lady got on as well. But Lorna was standing next to the doors, and me and my man held back.

'And we got it right. As the doors closed, she stepped off the train, and walked through to the westbound line. She caught out the cops and my lady.

'She did exactly the same again, and this time caught my guy. I had hung back. I always carry a disguise. You know, like hat, glasses and moustache. So I kept well back and hoped she wouldn't recognise me. But the station was pretty busy.

'She went through to the eastbound platform again. I had a fifty-fifty choice. On or not? I chose on, and that was right.

'She got off the train at Bank station. I was about twenty yards behind her in the crowd, heading for the escalators, and she just disappeared. I lost her.

'I retraced my steps and found a 'No Entry' passage going off to the left that she must have used. People were flooding down towards the Central Line platforms. But some folks were going into this passage. And I did the same. Came out at the Northern Line platforms.

'Now, Bank Station is one of the most complex on the network. It serves five separate lines. And so I lost her. No idea where she went.'

'Do you think she knew you were following her?'

'I don't think so. She never glanced back once. I just think that's the way she travels on the tube. Maybe she just assumes a constant tail. She came back to her flat around five o'clock.'

'Wow. Smart girl, huh?'

'So, I *think* the police are tapping her phone and tailing her. And that means they're suspicious. Can I now move on to what I don't know, but think what might be possible?'

'Sure. Go ahead.'

'Okay. I know gangs used this girl as a professional lure on two occasions. And probably on many others. That's how she can live in an expensive flat.

'That means she knows killers. So let's assume you're right for a moment. That she organised the attack as revenge for Dmitri chopping off her fingertip. But how did she know it was him?

'You said yourself the girl was unconscious when Dmitri loaded her into the taxi two years ago. And she remained that way until he dumped her. So she couldn't have recognised Andrei as Dmitri.

'She had only talked to Andrei twice before the fateful night. Once on the phone the previous night. But even if she picked up something on that call, I doubt she could organise such a hit in twenty-four hours.

'So it must be when they first met in May. He must have said something or did something that alerted her he was the man who maimed her.

'I've thought about it all weekend, and I can't come up with an answer to what that could be. Unless he told her direct. But he wouldn't do that.

'So, I'm stumped. And I'm coming to the conclusion that, even though everything we've talked about points to her as the organiser, I think that's maybe wrong. She couldn't have done it because she could never have got the link between Andrei and Dmitri.

'And it's also a hell of a big action to take for the loss of a fingertip. Don't you think?'

'Well, is she beautiful?'

'Yeah, I would say so.'

'Beautiful women hate any imperfections, Paul.'

'Maybe you're right. But if it's not business related, and it's a personal attack, then I think the solution may lie not with her, but with another aspect of his personal life we don't know about. What do you think?'

192

'Oh my goodness, Paul. Would need time to think about that, and go through all his personal papers again. I thought we were on the right track with her.'

'I know. What do you want me to do? Keep tailing her? Or what? Talk to your people here? Maybe they know something they're not telling you?'

'That's a good idea. I'll check this end again. Go and see Igor and Irina Dubov. Here's their number and address. I'll tell them to expect your call.

'But keep the tail on Lorna. I accept your logic, but there's too much pointing towards her to stop at this time. I agree though, we may still be missing something. So, I'll check this end again.'

'Okay. I'll keep going. Talk to you next week. Bye.'

Chapter 15. New Year's Day

Sandra sat beside Chuck on the sofa, listened to the radio, and waited for Big Ben to chime midnight. At the first stroke, she turned to him. 'Happy New Year, my darling. Hope it's a good one for us.'

'Yeah, honey. Happy New Year. Goodbye 1948. Hello 1949.' They kissed.

She jumped up. 'First, we need to let the old year out and the new year in.' She opened the doors on to the balcony and stepped out. Chuck joined her and they hugged. A cool, calm, still night. Ship's horns sounded on the Thames in the distance. A few car horns beeping. Sounds of music from other flats around them. 'Let's go back in.' She closed the doors behind her.

'Want your annual tot of whisky?'

'That would be nice, thanks.' He prepared two Scotch on the Rocks, and they linked arms as they toasted. 'To us.'

'Yeah, honey. To us.'

'Want a bit of mum's shortbread? First time in ten years she's made it.'

He took a bite. 'Mm. Delicious.'

'Better give her a quick call. . She'll be waiting.'

She called her mum and exchanged greetings. 'Right. Let's get on with the festivities.'

'Okay. Remind me, honey?'

'We're going down to Olivia's flat. She wants you as her first foot. Tall, dark and handsome for good luck.'

'Sounds good.'

Then across the hall to her new neighbour. She's throwing a party till three.'

'Do you know her?'

'I don't. But Olivia says she's a chorus girl in the show we're all going to tonight.'

'A chorus girl? In these flats?'

'Well, Olivia thinks she's from Dutch aristocracy.'

'Oh. So she enhances our status, not lowers it?'

Sandra chuckled. 'That's right.'

'Then what?'

'Grab some sleep. Lunch for the four of us at Wheeler's. Then a champagne river cruise. Then the show at the Hippodrome at night, called "High Button Shoes". A fast musical show set in New Jersey. Olivia says you'll like it.'

'She knows me that well? Is it a special show?'

'No, just the regular Saturday show.'

'Well, at least we'll see our chorus girl neighbour. What's her name?'

'Audrey Hepburn. Olivia reckons she won't be a chorus girl long. When she smiles the whole room lights up. Olivia says she could be a future star.'

'Really? Look forward to meeting her.'

***

They were at the coffee stage in Wheeler's when the head waiter approached her. Sandra looked up.

'Excuse me, ma'am. Phone call for you.'

She glanced round Chuck, Olivia and Digby, and shrugged. 'Sorry. Duty calls.'

The waiter showed her to a booth next to his desk, and she picked up the phone. 'Hello?'

'Hello, ma'am. Sorry to bother you.' *Her number two, Brian. On call for the day.* 'I need your advice.'

'Okay, Brian. And a happy New Year to you.'

'Oh, of course, ma'am. And to you.'

'Tell me what's happened.'

'We've had a break in the Andrei Rykov case.'

195

'Wow. Good news?'

'I think so, ma'am. We picked up another call this morning from this Glasgow guy who's called Lorna a couple of times in the last three months. Always on a Saturday morning. Never use names. She always goes out to meet him, and shakes off her tails every time. So, we've no idea who he is or where they meet.

'On each occasion, we've traced the call to a phone box near Hammersmith station. But it takes a few minutes to do the trace, and by the time a patrol gets there, the man's gone. That's why we now park a patrol near that phone box every Saturday.

'But this morning's call was different. They used names for the first time. Quote, "Happy New Year, Cathie. Just wanted to let you know I asked Helen to marry me, and she said yes. Oh, that's brilliant, Rab. I'm so pleased for you. Happy New Year to you both. Thanks Cathie. See you."

'We alerted our patrol, but they said no one had used that phone box in the last half-hour. So we traced the call to another phone box half-a-mile away.

'They raced there, and found a fight in progress next to it. A thirty-two year old man defending himself from an attack by three drunken young yobs trying to rob him.

'By this time, the yobs were broken and bruised on the pavement. And then another police car and an ambulance pulled up. Called by a neighbour who saw what happened.

'But the man didn't want to press charges. Just three stupid wee boys, full of themselves with drink, and picked the wrong target.

'Then the neighbour got involved. Said that he'd seen the yobs attack the man as he left the phone box, and the police should lock them up. There was too much of that sort of thing in the area now.

'Our patrol took the man into their car, and questioned him on his phone call. He said he had phoned his mother in Glasgow.

'They asked if he'd phoned anyone else, and he said no. So the patrol brought him here for further questions. He speaks with a Glasgow accent. His name is Robert Dunn, otherwise known as Rab. And, best of all, ma'am, he's a five foot six plumber.'

'Wow. Now that's *very* interesting, Brian.'

'So the way I see it, ma'am. We have a direct link between Lorna and the Russian, Andrei, on a date. We now have a link between Lorna and a five foot six plumber, who could be Andrei's attacker. What we need now is the link between Rab and Andrei.

'I'd like to now pull in Lorna for questioning again, and get a warrant to search both their properties to find the missing link. What do you say?'

'Go ahead, Brian. My authority. Potential murder charge for Rab. Accessory to murder for Lorna. Well done. Find out all you can about Rab. See you tomorrow to agree the way forward, and get it started on Monday.'

'Thank you, ma'am. See you then.'

She went back to the table with a big smile. Chuck looked up. 'Good news, honey?'

'Yeah. Just might be.'

***

Nadya checked her watch. Time to get the family round the dinner table. Her maid approached. 'Phone call from London, madam. Mr Paul Lynch,'

She made her way through to her study and picked up the phone. 'Hello? Paul?'

'Hello Nadya. Happy New Year to you.'

'Same to you. Why the call?'

'My team watching the girl, Lorna, has just told me a bunch of police have taken her from her flat, and seem to be searching it.'

'Do we know why?'

'We don't, Nadya. And we think it might be Special Branch. And I've got no contacts there.'

'Oh, that's a pity.'

'I'll try to find out what's happened though, and get back to you. Just thought you'd like to know.'

'Thanks, Paul. Appreciate it.'

'You're welcome, Nadya.'

She hung up. *Mmm. What had happened over there? Something to do with Dmitri's death? Hope so. The family needed closure.* She went back to her party.

***

Sandra and Chuck waved goodbye as Olivia and Digby entered the lift to go down to their flat.

She sighed. 'A long day, but a good day, huh?'

'Yeah. Great day. Enjoyed all of it.'

'What did you like most?'

'You singing at the party. A big surprise.'

'Well, with that showbiz crowd, everyone had to do a turn. And that was the only song I knew.'

'Inspired choice, though. Auld Lang Syne. Got them all singing. They were a good crowd.'

'Yeah. They also loved your 'Beautiful Dreamer'

'Well, they tolerated it.'

'Oh, don't do yourself down. They enjoyed it.'

'That girl, Alma Cogan, though. She can sure belt out a song. And she was in the chorus line tonight as well Good show too. What did you think of Audrey?'

'Thought Olivia's description was spot on. They're not going to be chorus girls long. Anyway, now we've tidied up, I think it's time for bed.'

'Right, agree with that.'

Ten minutes later she cuddled into him. 'Loved being with you all day, darling.'

'Me too.'

She lifted her nightie, rolled onto him, and savoured him manipulating her sensitive spots in his special way until they climaxed together. 'My darling.'

'My special girl.' She cuddled into him again and held him close. 'By the way, honey, today was also a red letter day for something else.'

She opened one eye. 'What's that?'

'Today, the law changed here. You no longer lose your nationality when you marry a foreigner. You can now stay British.'

She opened the other eye, and smiled. 'Really?'

'Yeah. It's true. But take our loving as a metaphor for our life. You lead the way wherever you want, and I'll love you to bits as I follow you.'

She kissed him. 'My darling man,' and cuddled into him again. *Why did he say that? Did he want to get married? She hadn't even thought about it. Loved her job and independence. Relished being in control of her life and finances. Loved him dearly. But didn't need a certificate to prove it. And no desire for children. Couldn't really be happier. Just enjoy the present.*

Chapter 16. Aftermath Two

The pressure on Sandra built during the following week. On Wednesday, she called a meeting with Brian Walker, her number two, and Gilbert Green, her best prosecutor, to discuss their position on the case.

'Calman called me this morning. Usual approach. Two innocent clients. And we're on a fishing trip. He's advised them to give "no comment" answers. We should release them now. Or charge them.

'He says the girl had two dates with the victim. She knows nothing about him. Never met him before. Yet we think she's complicit in his murder? Why?

'And the man as a murderer? Nonsense. He has one conviction for theft, and a rock-solid alibi.

'And he's right. We can't hold them forever. So, what do we do? Any forensics yet, Brian?'

'They've just come back this morning, ma'am. The glove fibres from the victim's coat match those on the gloves from Rab's home. Both tainted with plumber's putty. But the fibres didn't come from his gloves. They're new gloves, and haven't lost any fibres yet. Must have changed them in the last month.'

Sandra grimaced. 'Shit.'

'But the biggest problem we have, ma'am, is Rab's alibi. Rab and the three women, one of them his new fiancée, occupy the four flats in their house. All four of them go to greyhound racing every Wednesday night, play solo whist every Thursday night, and go to the pub for a sing-song every Friday night.

'And that includes Thursday 2nd September. They played cards till after ten, had a cup of tea, then to bed. He was never at Piccadilly Circus tube station.'

'Shit again. Are the women credible, Brian?'

'Yeah. Typical wee cockneys. Loved by all. Would make great witnesses.'

Sandra sighed. 'What do you think, Gilbert?'

'Well, Brian's right, of course. Big problem there. As I see it, we need to prove three links.

'First, the easy one. Between Lorna and Rab. That's the phone call.

'Second, the more difficult one. Between Rab and Andrei. Now made impossible by Brian's two points. We need to prove Rab wasn't with them that night by proving where he was. And that's not easy.

'Third, the even more difficult one. Between Lorna and Andrei/Dmitri. Two parts to this question. How did she know he was Dmitri? And if the attack was revenge for cutting off her finger tip, would any jury believe she would murder someone in response?

'To be honest, Sandra, I have a problem with this case. Sorry. Over to you.'

'Well, I also wondered how Lorna could recognise Andrei as Dmitri. Two years ago, after the kidnap, she said the man who bundled her into a taxi shouted to the driver, "You dash, or something like it". I've got it on file, though now she can't remember it, so she says.

'I've researched the words the attacker shouted at the tube station, and I think he shouted "Udachi" as he pushed Andrei off the platform. A Russian word that means "best of luck" or "Godspeed"

'Now, Dmitri had a girlfriend here, who left London after the Russian swap affair, and now lives in Torquay. She told me Dmitri used that exact word every time he parted with someone. A family habit, he said. And she's willing to testify on this point if required.

'We now know Dmitri injected Lorna with a fast-acting knock-out drug to kidnap her, but I believe she heard him shout that word before she went under.

'I talked yesterday to a professor of psychology at London University about this. He said it's possible in a traumatic event, for the brain to retain a vivid memory of actions and words during it.

'He says the long-term memory has three elements, procedural, semantic and episodic, and the latter would retain that shouted word. He'd testify to that effect.

'So, I think, when Andrei left her on the first date, he said that word to her as he always did. And it triggered her episodic memory. She realised he was the man who kidnapped her two years ago.

'And because she's a sly, vicious bitch under her beautiful veneer, she went straight for murder. And got Rab to shout that word to make us think of a Russian link. I think she's been involved in murders in the past, though I can't prove it. Could we use any of that?'

Gilbert took a deep breath. 'Well, it would explain how she knew Andrei was Dmitri okay, with back-up from the professor. I think it ticks that link. So, we're left with Rab and his alibi. How do we break that?'

'That's our biggest problem. And Josh Calman drills all his witnesses so they're perfect. Any ideas, Brian?'

'No, ma'am. They were adamant he was with them that night. He's not a violent man, and we've no evidence on him from the tube station.'

'Shit. With no photos showing criminals in action, we rely on fingerprints as our only unique identifier. And we can only get them from hard surfaces. Roll on the day when we can get prints from clothes or skin. That would be a game changer for us.

'I hate giving up. But if we have to, let's not reveal what we know. Then we can come back to it again. Go ahead, Brian. Release them.'

***

Nadya lifted the phone. 'Hello, Paul?'

'Hi Nadya. Just to let you know, the girl Lorna has returned to her flat. The police have released her.'

'Any further details?'

'I called her to follow up my previous call, and to wish her a Happy New Year. Asked her if she had any further contact with the police, but she said she hadn't.

'Now, I didn't want to reveal what we knew. But she must have cleared any questions they asked. And she probably had a good lawyer.

'She's still seems an innocent party, though. Did you ever have another look at whether Dmitri upset anyone else over there?'

'We did, Paul. Dmitri took tough decisions with some of our customers here in the past. But we had no links to any Borodin, and we always tried to smooth over any problems that arose.

'And, anyway, we keep our UK business a secret over here. So, if anyone local was upset, they'd more likely take action here than in the UK.

'So, we're a hundred percent certain the attack was not business related. It had to be personal. You cleared the girl, Jill Graham. We can't find any other personal contact. So, by elimination, Lorna must be involved.'

'What do you want me to do, then?'

'Oh, we've gone as far as we can, Paul. Let's bring it to a close. Finish it now. How much do we owe you?'

'You're still four pounds in credit.'

'Right. So why don't you treat your wife to a nice meal on us as a thank you? We've enjoyed working with you, Paul, and we'll get back to you if we need to.'

'Okay, Nadya. Thanks. Happy with that. Bye.'

'Goodbye.'

***

A week later, Sandra had her monthly meeting with Eliot Forbes, from MI5, and Pascal Barnes, the Anglo-French head of Interpol in the UK, to discuss current complex cases where they each had a role.

Ten minutes in, and Gayle, her secretary, came in with a note. 'CI Walker needs to see you. Urgent.'

'Could you excuse me a minute, lads? Something I need to deal with.'

Brian stood in Gayle's office. 'Sorry to disturb you, ma'am. Ray Todd from the Met just called. They found Lorna Mitchell dead this morning. Fell from the roof garden at her block of flats. Drunk as a skunk. Signs that she slipped and stumbled over a low wall. Just thought you'd like to know.'

'Oh, my God. Poor girl.' She felt tears well in her eyes. 'When did it happen?'

'They think around three-thirty. Found by a milkman at six. But no witnesses so far.'

She grimaced. 'I'll be another hour or so. Find out all you can and we'll meet then.'

'Right, ma'am.'

She went back into her office. Eliot looked up, concerned. 'Everything okay, Sandra?'

'Ah, no. Just heard one of my favourite customers died this morning. Fell from her roof garden in the early hours while drunk. Horrible accident.

Pascal leaned forward. 'Sure it was an accident?'

'How do you mean?'

'Well, did she have any Russian links?'

'Yes, she did. Is that significant?'

'Could be. Last week, we had our monthly meeting of West Europe heads. In the last three months, we've seen three people fall from high windows or roofs. In Brussels, Amsterdam and Paris. The only common thread? Each had a Russian link that went sour.

'We think there's a bunch of ex-NKGB guys, with contracts from top Russians, getting rid of people that crossed swords with them.

'That's their modus operandi. Enter the country. Find the person. Fill them with alcohol. Up on the roof or high window. Do the deed. And out of the country before they find the body. And never caught.

'We've dubbed it Russian Revenge. And I think you should consider this, Sandra. We'll help you all we can.'

'Thanks Pascal. Let's discuss it after the meeting.'

Bloody hell. Bloody Russians. But let's get through this meeting first.

***

Sandra arrived home to find Chuck already there. She kissed him. 'Good day?'

'Yeah. Two return trips to Paris. Everything on time. Good day. How about yourself, honey? I've got your drink here.' He handed her the glass. 'Cheers.'

She flopped on her sofa and plumped a cushion behind her back. 'Cheers. Shit day, to be honest.'

'Don't often hear that, honey. Tell me about it.'

'Remember a couple of years ago? The girl at the cottage in Rhu?'

'Yeah. Blew the whistle on the Russians? Went into witness protection?'

'That's her. Found dead this morning. Fell from the roof garden at her block of flats. On the face of it, a tragic accident.

'But I had a meeting with the head of Interpol today, and he told me there's been a rash of similar cases in Western Europe. And they're no accident. In each case, they crossed swords with Russians. He calls it the Russian Revenge.'

'Bloody hell. And is this the same thing?'

'Could well be. The gold and diamond butterfly brooch the Russian gave her is missing. But we've no witnesses and no evidence. So we don't really know.'

'The Russians kidnapped me too. They dumped me and the girl behind Selfridges. Am I at risk too?'

'No. You were just a pawn in the swap game. You didn't cross swords with them in that sense.'

'Glad to hear it. So how did she upset them?'

'You know I don't talk about my cases. Just let's say it's possible she was involved in the death of a Russian. And paid the price.'

'Geez. It's a murky world you work in, honey.'

'Yeah, it is. And it doesn't usually affect me. But I knew this girl better than any other crook I've handled. And to some extent, liked her.

'I think most people find life tough at times. They need someone beside them to help navigate their way through. A kind of Captain, if you will. Maybe a spouse, family member, or close friend.

'Lorna had her brother. Probably at her most successful then. But she lost him. He went to prison.

'She then had her Swiss banker. But more or less lost him when he went back to Switzerland. She then tried to land Sir Anthony, but he turned her down.

'I think it left her rudderless, and she made mistakes that led to her downfall.

'I'm so grateful to have you at my side, darling. You're *my* Captain. Just like your aircraft, you help me fly. Keep me balanced. Keep me content. Help me land safely. And that's bliss.' She leaned over and kissed him. 'Love you, darling. So glad I found you.'

'Love you too, honey. Just perfect for me too.'

A Note from James Hume

Thank you so much for reading Finding the Captain, the sequel to Avenging the Captain, and Book 3 in the Captain Trilogy. I hope you enjoyed it.

If you have a moment, please leave an honest review at Amazon or Goodreads. Even if it's only a line or two, it would be *very* much appreciated.

I welcome contact from my readers. If you'd like to hear about new releases in advance, send a brief email to james@jameshumeauthor.com

Or if you want to comment on any part of the storyline, then please also send an email and I'll happily respond. But first, check out other readers' comments below to see if I've covered your subject there.

I won't share your email with anyone else, nor clutter your inbox. I'll only contact you to respond or when a new release is imminent.

James Hume

Some Notes on the World War 2 Period

In my storylines, I use the technology of the time as authentically as possible, based on family and friends' experiences, (since I was just a young boy during ww2), or from deep research.

Like most authors, I also use artistic licence to help tell an interesting story, and provide my readers with the best possible reading experience.

However, some readers challenge me on aspects of the storyline that don't ring true to them. In a couple of cases, where they proved their point, I've changed the text so other readers don't have that same experience.

But most of the issues they raise <u>could</u> have happened as described in the story. Let me illustrate with some of their challenges.

Tape Recorders?

The 1930s was a decade of great technical innovation, though it's hard for us to see the full impact looking back from today.

Recording machines using magnetic wire were available from the mid-thirties, and used by law enforcement for evidence gathering. The end of the decade saw portable versions of these machines available. But their use was largely limited to special applications, such as broadcasting or law enforcement, through the 1940s.

The widespread use of recording machines only took place after the war with the development of magnetic tape. So I agree, tape recorders were not available at the time of the story.

In my first draft, I used the term 'wire recorders' to describe the machines of the time. That is technically correct, but has an entirely different meaning today.

Therefore, to avoid confusion, I changed that term to 'recorders' or 'recording machines' for those machines that used magnetic wire. But not tape recorders.

CIA?

During World War 2, US President Franklin Roosevelt created the Office of Strategic Services (OSS) as an intelligence service modelled on the British MI6.

Shortly after the end of the war, President Harry Truman transformed the OSS into the National Intelligence Authority. Its operational extension was known as the Central Intelligence Group (CIG), which was the direct predecessor of the CIA.

In mid-1947, President Truman transformed the above organisations into the National Security Council and the Central Intelligence Agency (CIA). The latter provides mainly overseas intelligence for the President and Cabinet of the US.

In the early timeline of the story therefore, the relevant US intelligence service was the CIG. However, because the CIA is now so well known internationally, I have used artistic licence to avoid confusing my readers, and refer to the relevant intelligence operations as CIA.

USAAF Base, Prestwick?

The USAAF base at Prestwick closed as an operational base by the end of 1945. However, some facilities were retained to use Prestwick's fog-free status as the key transit point for US military flights to and from Europe.

British Married Women's Nationality?

In the previous story, Sandra and Chuck fall in love, and want to get married. But can't do so because, under UK law at the time, a British woman marrying an alien, (in this case, an American), automatically lost her British nationality and took her husband's. Because Sandra wanted to retain her job in law enforcement, she needed British nationality. They therefore decided not to get married. Some readers have challenged this position.

Now, for most couples, this quirk of British law did not pose a problem. During the WW2 period, over 70,000 British women married US servicemen. But because the US Immigration process is so complex, and can take a year or more to complete and gain US citizenship, 'GI brides' sometimes found themselves stranded in a legal limbo when things went wrong in their marriage during that period. Neither legally British nor legally American. In fact, legally stateless. Now Britain and most other countries had signed up to the Hague Convention in the early 1930s, to banish statelessness, so in such cases, the British government stepped in to help these women as though they were British.

The basic principle that a woman's nationality followed her husband's was established in Britain by the 1870 Naturalisation Act.

The British Nationality and Status of Aliens (BNSA) Act of 1914 re-enacted this principle by stating, 'The wife of a British subject shall be deemed to be a British subject, and the wife of an alien should be deemed an alien.'

The passage of the BNSA Amendment Act in 1933 gave effect to the Hague Convention in Britain. Its aim was to remove the causes of statelessness. It restated the above principle as in the 1914 Act, but added, 'Where a woman has married an alien, and was at the time of her marriage a British subject, she shall not, by reason only of her marriage, be deemed to have ceased to be a British subject unless, by reason of her marriage, she acquired the nationality of her husband.' This meant that the above principle still applied by default, but if the woman lost her alien nationality after marriage, she would not be stateless as before, but deemed to be a British subject. However, the British woman still could not elect to retain her British nationality on marrying an alien. Her legal position on marriage had not changed.

Despite intense debate over this period, particularly from feminist groups complaining about how this nationality principle treated men and women differently, successive British governments refused to change it, to uphold the unity of the family, and because they wanted to preserve the integrity of the British Empire. Within the Empire, all Dominion citizens were deemed British first, and Canadian or Australian, etc, second. So their women were caught in the same marriage trap.

It was only when Canada announced the Canadian Citizenship Act in 1945, (without referring first to Britain), that allowed their women to retain their local Canadian nationality on marriage to an alien, that the dam began to break. This was quickly followed by the similar New Zealand Amendment Act and the Australian Amending Act in 1946. These Acts effectively destroyed the Empire-wide allegiance to the British Crown.

The UK passed its own Nationality Act in 1948, coming into force on 1st January, 1949, providing finally that marriage would have no effect on a British woman's nationality. Provision 14 stated, 'A woman who, having before the commencement of this Act married any person, ceased on that marriage … to be a British subject, shall be deemed … to have been a British subject immediately before … this Act.'

So, our couple could have married at the later time of the story. However, since the 1920s, female police officers in the UK had to resign on marriage.

This was rescinded in England and Wales in 1946, and in Scotland in 1968. But many women of the 1920s and 1930s like Sandra, were inspired by Amelia Earhart to be proud of their independence. And so, when Chuck hinted about marriage at New Year, 1949, she backed off, preferring to keep the status quo.

(Main Source: Subject to Empire: Married Women and the British Nationality and Status of Aliens Act by M. Page Baldwin on JSTOR website)

Soviet Spies?

In this story, our fictional Russian bankers provide secret funds for real-life Soviet spies – the Portland spy ring and Klaus Fuchs - still to be revealed at that time. Now, somebody did pay them, but the links in the story solely reflect the author's imagination.

Psychological Thriller?

Compared with my first two stories, (Hunting Aquila and Chasing Aquila), my three later stories, (Killing the Captain), (Avenging the Captain), and this one (Finding the Captain) are much more psychological in tone. The characters are driven not just by events, but by inner motivations, as part of the human condition.

I hope you accept these points, and they allay any concerns you may have over the rigour of the story. I always aim for accuracy, particularly in this story, on the coverage of the above aspects at the time.

The storylines are fiction, but <u>could</u> have happened. That's how I use artistic licence.

I learn so much from my readers, and love to capture every nuance of their reading experience if I can. So, please contact me with any points you wish to make.

See below for my other books. Happy reading,

James Hume

Hunting Aquila (An intriguing WW2 spy drama, with a twist)

During World War 2, Churchill stumbles across a leak of vital information from the UK to the enemy and calls in Commander Jonathan Porritt to catch the mole. Porritt has no leads until Jane, a young British translator, unwittingly gets caught up with a German spy trying to flee the country. Can Porritt use his Special Branch teams in Glasgow, Yorkshire, London and Belfast to rescue Jane and smash the undercover spy organisation before Churchill's invasion plans get leaked?

This deftly plotted, action-packed thriller is full of twists and turns. Carefully weaving fact and fiction, it provides powerful and intriguing lessons that still apply in today's changing world.

"Great story and premise. Many engaging characters. Once I began reading it the only time I stopped was when I had to charge my Kindle. I hate to compare authors, but if I didn't know Hume wrote this, I'd guess Ken Follett did. The novel is that good." (Bill Hoyler)

"Well written spy novel. Grabs you from beginning to end. Great characters, both good and bad." (JW)

Link to amazon.com - https://amzn.to/38Kysrk

Link to amazon.co.uk - https://amzn.to/3iPmKjU

Chasing Aquila (Sequel to Hunting Aquila)

Just after World War 2, Superintendent Sandra Maxwell, Head of Special Branch in the West of Scotland, checks if a suspicious death in Glasgow is linked to Aquila, a German spy organisation that flourished in the UK during the war. She finds that Aquila has now morphed into a sinister new organisation. Can she and her colleagues in London catch the killer by chasing him across Holland and Germany, capture the head of the organisation, and smash their new activities before they spread to every major UK city?

This deftly plotted, action-packed thriller is full of twists and turns. Carefully weaving fact and fiction, it provides powerful and intriguing lessons that still apply in today's changing world.

"I enjoyed this as much as the previous one. The detail of the considerations by Special Branch, Civil Service, Army and criminals mesh together to complete the plot. Chasing Aquila is full, rounded, with real characters having real emotions, living real lives and doing real jobs. With the historical information as a background, this is an all-round good read." (Jonathan Pedlar)

Link to amazon.com - https://amzn.to/2ObOMrQ

Link to amazon.co.uk - https://amzn.to/2Cq8eyi

Killing the Captain (A post-WW2 crime drama, with a twist)

Book 1 of the Captain Trilogy, in which a dispute between two businessmen in the UK escalates into two US CIA v Soviet stand-offs. This book sets the scene.

Just after World War 2, when partly deaf Adam Bryson lip reads a conversation between two businessmen planning an assassination in the UK, it sets off a series of events that involve Sandra Maxwell, Head of Special Branch in the West of Scotland, her colleagues in London, and Colonel Chuck Campbell, Head of the USAAF base in Scotland. Can she identify and save the target, capture the crooks and deal with the aftermath before anyone gets killed?

"A well-researched and accurate depiction of a rather difficult time for Britain. A good story, well told, and kept me busy reading! I have read all three of this sequence of stories and much look forward to the next one. Soon, I hope." (E.A.M)

"I really enjoyed reading this book. I read the last few chapters really slowly as I didn't want to reach the end. Great characters and story lines." (Alan)

Link to amazon.com - https://amzn.to/3gRPHKn

Link to amazon.co.uk - https://amzn.to/2ZWGVUo

Avenging the Captain (Sequel to Killing the Captain) (Prequel to this book)

Book 2 of the Captain Trilogy, in which a dispute between two businessmen in the UK escalates into two US CIA v Soviet stand-offs. This book has the first minor clash.

Just after World War 2, Gary West, Head of CIA Operations in Europe, is puzzled by sinister activities of staff at Soviet Embassies. Their latest seems to focus on Glasgow, Scotland. Can Sandra Maxwell, Head of Special Branch in the West of Scotland and her colleagues in London, help the CIA solve the puzzle, capture the crooks, and deal with the aftermath before anyone gets killed?

"Good story. Great sequel to Killing the Captain"(Cary)

"I enjoyed the characters and the plot. It was a fast-moving story with real-life twists and turns. I look forward to reading more stories by James Hume." (Rick)

"Mr Hume was able to transition through all three books without losing any of the players. Highly recommend these books." (Amazon Customer)

Link to amazon.com – https://amzn.to/3WD2Uec

Link to amazon.co.uk - https://amzn.to/3R7mZrW

Finding the Captain

Printed in Great Britain
by Amazon

21425304R00130